Stella & Ray

K. CRUZ

Stella & Ray

A Nuyorican Love Story

Charleston, SC
www.PalmettoPublishing.com

Stella & Ray

Copyright ©2023 by K. Cruz

First Edition

Hardcover ISBN: 979-8-8229-1073-7
Paperback ISBN: 979-8-8229-1074-4
eBook ISBN: 979-8-8229-1075-1

Dedication

My husband Luis—my rock. Thank you for your patience and support while I went on this journey with Stella and Ray. I love you.

Catherine, Genesis, and Annie—My girls and beta readers who fell in love with Stella and Ray as much as I did.

Korynn—My Kay since we were eight years old—xoxo

Ma, Pa (in heaven), Wela, Tio, and the rest of my family—thank you for always keeping me in line the Puerto Rican way. I love ha!

Chapter 1

"Ray, I love you, and I hope this move is everything you need," Stella told him, even though her heart was broken. She grabbed his face and looked into his eyes. "You go out there and kill this thing. You're going to do wonderful things. Move on with your life," she said, and as the words left her lips, they broke her. The thought of him with someone else consumed her with jealousy and anger, but it had to be done if he were to live his dream. They agreed the only way for him to truly concentrate was for him to be single and not feel bound to her while living in LA. She didn't want him feeling guilty for wanting to live. This move from New York to LA was difficult enough for Ray without having to worry about what Stella was doing. They decided breaking up was for the best.

"Stella, I've never loved anyone the way I love you, and I will never love anyone the way I love you," Ray said, holding her tight against him.

She whispered, "Neither will I."

His best friend, Sebastian Huerta, said, "Bro, we gotta go." He tapped Ray on the shoulder to separate them for a heartbeat. Seb leaned down and gave Stella a long, hard hug.

Stella held on to him too. "Seb, please take care of him for me." He nodded at her.

Ray came back to her, and they kissed one last time. "*Te quiero mucho*, my Stella" were the last words he said to her before letting her go to get on the plane heading for Los Angeles. He looked back at her one last time, and she kissed her two fingers and pointed at him. It was the last thing he saw before he walked on to the plane.

She felt her soul leave her body, and in that moment, she knew she would never know love like this again.

Chapter 2
Two years later

"I had a nice time," Stella said, trying to be polite and walking up to her front door. She put her key in the door and turned to open it. She turned back to face him. Jason Guerrero, her first date in two years, was six foot two, with short black hair, brown eyes, and glasses. He worked at a law firm and was an aspiring lawyer set to take his bar exam in a few months. He was slim but fit and in shape. He was nice enough, but Stella just wanted to be alone. Jason wasn't interested in anything she liked. All he talked about was law, and since she worked at a law office, she did not want to talk shop on her off time. She needed to accept the fact that she would never feel the way she once did and that you only fall in love once.

"So did I," he said, and he leaned down for a kiss, but Stella wasn't feeling it. She turned her head, and his face turned dark. "What the fuck, Stella?" he growled, and he grabbed her left arm.

"Ok, this is over," Stella said, trying to pull her arm away, but he had a firm grip on her and shoved her inside and kicked her door closed. She swung with her right fist and connected but barely moved him. He pulled his arm back and connected with the side of her face. It felt as if her face exploded, and she hit the floor.

"Dumb bitch thought she would embarrass me," she vaguely heard him say. Everything was happening so fast. He was on top of her, and she tried to swing again, but he caught her arm this time, and he slapped her twice. She felt him unbuttoning her pants, and she tried to swing again, but he just batted her away. She kicked her legs, but he was on top of her and had her pinned. When she kept moving, he hit her in the ribs, and she felt a crack, and this time she couldn't fight back. She felt her pants come down and his body invade hers. Her tears came down as she felt him ram into her. She tried to scream, and he slapped her again. After what felt like an eternity, he finally got off her, pulled his pants on, and left. She was on the floor a bloody mess. Stella just lay there. She couldn't believe this had just happened to her. Her cracked rib made it both difficult to move and difficult to breathe. She needed to get help, so she crawled to her bag and grabbed her phone. She dialed the one person she knew she could rely on.

Chapter 3
Two years later

"Oh, come on!!!" Stella yelled at the TV. She tended to yell when *Game of Thrones* or something along the same lines was on. These shows really got her emotions going. Sitting down with some gummy worms, wrapped under the covers with her golden Cavapoo dog, Brandy, there was nowhere else she would rather be on a Sunday night.

Stella had never had another date after the events of two years ago. She still had a tough time sleeping and would jump up in bed thinking he would show up again. She moved after that incident, afraid he would come back since he knew where she lived. There was only one person who knew what had happened to her, and that was her best friend, Kayla, because she had needed help afterward. Nobody else.

Stella Gomez was twenty-seven and had a full-time job and a good head on her shoulders. She worked as an executive assistant for one of the partners in a law firm for the past four years and was comfortable. As long as she could take care of Brandy and herself, she didn't need anything else. She moved from Brooklyn to an apartment in Manhattan, and although the apartment was small, it was home for now. It was the cheapest apartment she could find. It wasn't luxurious. Because she was from Brooklyn, it seemed like a step up. Her dream home was in the suburbs, away from the hustle and bustle of the city. She liked the city but much preferred to have a quiet life without hearing the ambulances, cops, fire trucks and buses going by every five minutes.

She was serious about four things in life—her family and friends, her dog, being good at her job, and fantasy shows. If she had Marvel and the rest of George R. R. Martin's shows and books, she was set for life. Loneliness never fazed her, not even around those sappy holidays. That was what Brandy was for. Brandy helped fill a void.

Stella's last and only meaningful relationship had lasted three years, and that had ended four years ago. She thought Ray Garcia was the love of her life. They liked the same music, movies, and games, they had easy conversations that would last for hours, he was a diligent worker, and the sex was mind blowing. He was six feet tall, with an athletic build, olive skin, and hazel eyes like hers. His hair was black and always short. He was everything Stella wanted. They had a passionate relationship until Ray got a job offer in California that was too good to pass up. He was a talented voice actor, and she always knew he would make it. Stella was crushed when he left and had closed her heart off after that. She knew she wouldn't follow him. They were young, and at the time she was not ready to leave her mother behind.

She turned the TV off and imagined what Ray was up to. She decided not to stay in contact with him as it was not in her best interest to hang on to something that couldn't be. She didn't want him to feel bound to her while he was out there, and she thought she wanted to move on with her life too.

She and Kayla were preparing for a long trip on Wednesday to San Diego, California, for Comic-Con. She was packed and ready to go. It was the first time she was traveling by plane, and she was looking forward to it. Excited and petrified. Ray was in LA, so she didn't have to worry about bumping into him in San Diego.

Stella was five foot two and weighed 115 pounds. She had hazel eyes and long brown hair that reached the middle of her back. She was pretty and could have had any guy she wanted if she would allow herself to open up. She had vowed never to feel that hurt of losing someone she loved again or to put herself in the position she had two years ago.

Kayla had had her hands full trying to get Stella back to a semblance of herself after Ray left—and then again two years ago. Seeing her battered and bruised in person was something Kayla would never forget. When she got to Stella's place, there was blood everywhere. Stella was trying to stand up but was having a hard time since she couldn't breathe right. Kay insisted they go to the emergency room. She also wanted Stella to call the police, but Stella was adamant about not doing that. All it would mean was that she would have to keep reliving this nightmare, and right now she just wanted to forget. She did have Kay take pictures of her bruises though. The doctors were not buying the "falling down the stairs" story, but they couldn't do anything if they didn't have the full story.

She had to stay away from her mother for two weeks while she healed. Her boss, Melissa Carlyle, a powerful woman, knew something was up. They had developed a close relationship, and when Stella told her she needed some time, Melissa said ok. Stella worked from home during those two weeks. When Stella returned to the office, she felt eyes on her and the new scar she had above her brow, especially from Melissa. If Melissa noticed it, she didn't say anything. It was painful to think about. But the nightmares Stella had were still fresh. She saw his face in her dreams every night.

She went to her mother's house on Tuesday to drop Brandy off. "Ay, *Dios mio*. Ma, the odds are zero. He's in LA. I will be in San Diego," Stella said, rolling her eyes at her mom, Sandra, who was hoping for them to reconnect. Sandra knew it had devastated Stella when Ray had left.

"Hey, you just never know. *Uno nunca sabe!*" Sandra said it in English and Spanish to make sure Stella understood. "Things happen. He liked the same things you did. He can show up there too." Her mom loved him. Everybody loved him.

Stella didn't want to imagine the scene if she did see him. She was a different person now. And he was a different person now. They both had their own lives. Out of curiosity, she would google and check his voice credits. There was the Netflix show that he had left New York for and one more. She would look at his picture, imagining what it would be like if she had gone with him. The last thing on her mind for this trip was Ray. And the first thing on her mind for this trip, even though she hated to admit it, was Ray. He had always been her safe space, and she both needed and missed it. The events of two years ago had confirmed the fact that Stella should have left with him.

Chapter 4

The six-hour flight felt long, but they watched a couple of movies on the plane. Stella did not want to admit how terrified of flying she was and would continue to be after all the turbulence on this flight! They landed, got their suitcases, and made their way to the hotel. They were able to catch a cab quickly. Stella let out a breath once they were inside the cab.

"Thank God that stupid flight is over! I'm never flying again," Stella said, and then she remembered she had to get back home in five days. She slapped her hand across her forehead. Kayla laughed.

"It wasn't that bad! You're exaggerating," Kayla said, still laughing.

Stella rolled her eyes—"Yes, the fuck it was!"—and they both laughed.

They had been friends for twelve years, since high school, and had maintained their friendship even after high school, which is when most people lose the friends they think they'll have forever. Kayla Smith was that one friend who always had Stella's back, and Stella always had Kayla's back. Kayla had a small family, and so did Stella. They gravitated toward each other as sisters quickly.

Stella and Kay were both excited to take in the scenes of San Diego as well as enjoy the hell out of

Comic-Con. While Stella was light skinned and on the shorter side, Kayla was her opposite, standing at five foot seven, with darker skin and beautiful model features. Her dark Costa Rican skin was smooth and blemish free. She was thick in all the right places.

They arrived at the Marriott Marquis Marina hotel, and they had a beautiful marina view from their room.

"This place is so beautiful," Kayla said walking around and taking in the ambiance of the room. It was a nice size, with two queen beds, a fifty-inch flat-screen TV, and a bathroom with a rain-head shower. Stella took out her Bluetooth speaker and placed it on the small table next to the window. She connected her phone to the speaker and "*Mi Gente*" by J. Balvin, Willy William & Beyonce came on. They started putting all their clothes away, while dancing and singing around the room. With five days' worth of wardrobe put away, they lay on one of the beds and started preparing for the show the next day. These shows were too big to tackle in one day. They broke it up into four different areas, so they didn't overdo it all in any given day.

When it got dark, the view from their room was amazing. There were buildings that were all lit up, and it was reminiscent of Manhattan but on a much smaller scale. A more peaceful scale. By the time they finished their planning, they were exhausted. Comic-Con was the next day, and they wanted to be ready. After going to two Comic Cons in New York, they knew they had long days ahead of them and would need to rest. They decided to order room service and just pig out in the room. Stella was having a hard time sleeping after they ate so she went to sit next to the window. Everything was so peaceful, and she didn't want to go to sleep and rock the boat with her dreams. She barely got any sleep as it was just so she wouldn't have to see Jason's face.

Stella started thinking about her father, Ruben, who had passed away right before she met Ray. She always thought her dad would have loved Ray, just like her mom did.

He got cancer of the prostate and didn't make it more than two years after his diagnosis. He was only thirty-nine and Sandra was shattered after his death. They were together for twenty years before his diagnosis and Sandra always said Ruben was the love of her life. Stella remembered their relationship fondly. They rarely fought and when they did, it was over quickly. They always said that there was nothing that could tear them apart and they were right, up until the doctor delivered the devastating news that he didn't have long to live. Everything was a blur after that. He was in and out of the hospital and his final admission to the hospital, Sandra and Stella knew he wouldn't be coming home. He was tired of fighting, and they didn't blame him. They stood with him day and night until his last breath. Stella always wondered what life would be like if he was still around. Would he be proud of her? What his advice would have been when Ray left? Would she open up and tell him what Jason did to her? She closed her eyes knowing she would never have answers to these questions.

Stella finally lay down at 2:00 a.m. and closed her eyes. When she opened them, she saw a tall figure standing over her. "Did you miss me, Stella?" the figure asked. It's a dream Stella, wake up, she tried to tell herself. The figure leaned down toward her slowly and Stella was paralyzed with fear until Jason's face was visible and he touched her. She jolted awake in the bed, sweating. Fuck, she thought. This is exactly why she didn't want to go to sleep. Kayla had suggested she go to therapy, but she didn't want to discuss this with anyone. Maybe it was time to finally find a therapist when she got back to New York. It was time to face this demon head on and not let it take over her life anymore.

Chapter 5

The next morning started at 6:00 a.m. It was game day, and they started getting ready. These conventions always felt like marathons you had to mentally prepare for. Stella wore a white Yankees pinstriped jersey, unbuttoned, with a white tank top underneath showing her midriff, along with tight blue jeans and a pair of white and navy-blue Jordan 4s. Her hair was up in a high ponytail whose length reached down the middle of her back, and she wore hoop earrings. Not one for makeup, she put a little foundation on and some eyeliner. After all, she had to look presentable for pictures!

Kayla wore a tight white Star Wars T-shirt with a deep V-neck that showed off her busty chest. She also wore jeans and sneakers. That was pretty much the uniform from New York and comfort was key. They were ready to go.

They arrived at 8:30 a.m. The show opened at 9:00 a.m., and the place was packed already. The buzz was electric, and the girls were so excited. Aside from the convention, there were some cute guys too. Kayla was definitely looking to have a fun time. Stella laughed to herself. Maybe she should open up a bit too. Make this once-in-a-lifetime trip something to really remember with a short fling. Yeah right, she thought. Never doing that again.

They decided to start at the back of the convention center today and work their way forward little by little every day. They had their bag for goodies in their hands and their badge around their neck. Looking around, Stella saw the Capcom booth and they headed for it. There was a giant Megaman statue in the corner. Stella and Kay took silly selfies in front of it. They continued walking and found the Nintendo booth. They both almost lost their shit when they saw giant statues of Mario, Luigi and Link. They considered themselves Nintendo freaks and weren't afraid to show it. They started running back and forth to all the statues and took more selfies. They noticed two guys watching them but paid them no mind. They continued taking pictures and admiring everything on display. Eventually, the guys came over and introduced themselves as Branden and Peter.

"So you guys like Nintendo stuff?" Peter asked and Kayla started eyeing him up and down. From his untucked shirt, to his beat-up sneakers and his unshaven face. The guy looked so sloppy and was trying to talk to women? Branden on the other hand, was more put together. His gray shirt and jeans were neatly pressed. His sneakers looked like he bought them just for this show and were brand new. Everything about him said professional.

"Yea we do," Kayla responded and kept walking with Stella next to her.

Branden positioned himself on the opposite side of Kayla and asked if he could get her number. Kayla gave him the once over again and said, "Sure." As Branden was talking to Kayla, Peter was trying to get on Stella's side and Stella kept moving away from him. He wouldn't go away and all she wanted to do was look at this particular exhibit in peace. Kayla gave Branden her number and they finally went away.

When Branden and Peter were far enough away, Stella took a breath. "What the fuck, man," she said with a giggle, and they started laughing. "Did you see what he looked like? And he's trying to pick women up when he looks like he didn't even take a damn shower!" Stella said laughing.

"Girl, I gave him the only dirty look. Dirtier than he looked," Kayla said and they doubled over in laughter. This is exactly what they needed. A break from real life for a little while.

After a few hours of walking, they were ready to sit down. Kayla had gotten a few phone numbers from guys while standing in lines for autographs. They grabbed a bite to eat and found a place on the floor to sit and stuff their faces. Stella had to use the bathroom. She went while Kayla was busy posting pictures on Instagram. On the way to the bathroom, Stella got sidetracked by some artists displaying their artwork.

There was one that was exhibiting drawings of Nintendo characters and he had a great sketch of Link from Zelda: Breath of the Wild. She would have to come back and buy that piece before she left.

Stella's urge to use the bathroom was stronger now and she needed to find it ASAP. She walked away from the artists' booth and started walking briskly in search of the bathroom. Finally, she saw the sign for it.

Chapter 6

Stella was pumping with adrenaline as she turned the corner to reach the bathroom when she felt someone's big body knock the wind out of her. She stumbled back and was caught by strong hands before she fell. When she looked up, she lost her breath again. The wall she had thought she hit was Ray. What are the freakin' odds? she said to herself.

They stared at each other for what felt like forever before Stella noticed a tall blond girl standing next to him. She tried to compose herself. She smiled and said, "Hey, Ray. So sorry about that. I'm still clumsy," half laughing.

His mouth turned up in a smile. He was still perfect. A little more mature looking since the last time they had seen each other, which suited him well. His hair was still short. But he had a goatee and beard, and his upper body was more muscular than it had been when she last saw him. His shirt was tight and she could see the outline of his chest and stomach. Stella had to refrain from fanning herself.

Ray looked her up and down quickly and said, "No, it's my fault. I wasn't paying attention." He reached down to give her a small hug. "It's been a long time." He looked at her and she noticed when his eyes landed on the scar above her brow.

"Yeah, it has," she said, trying not to look directly at him or smell him because he smelled delicious.

"This is my girlfriend, Meghan." He made the introduction with an awkward smile. Meghan did not look pleased. "Meghan, this is my friend from New York, Stella." And from her facial expression, Meghan knew exactly who Stella was. Meghan gave Stella a once-over before saying, "Hey," almost rolling her eyes. This bitch, thought Stella.

Before Stella could say hey back, she heard somebody say, "Holy shit, is that Stella??" from behind Ray. It was his good friend Sebastian. He pushed his way past Ray to give Stella a big hug. Stella was caught off guard as he hugged her tight and picked her up. Stella tightened up, and Sebastian noticed. He looked at her, and she gave her best fake smile. They had done this a million times before, and Stella could tell from Seb's expression, he knew something was different. He put her back down on the floor. She also saw him notice the scar by her brow. Stella quickly started talking to deflect.

"Oh man, Sebastian, it's been a long time!! You look great!"

"So do you. Wowza. Twenty-seven is looking good on you, woman!" They laughed. Meghan had a raised eyebrow watching this interaction with Seb and Stella. She had her arms crossed and frown. Almost in a pout. She looked mad at all the attention Stella was getting.

Out of the corner of her eye, Stella saw Meghan get close to Ray's face and kiss his neck. She then wrapped her arms around Ray's stomach and looked in Stella's direction with an evil smirk. Seb continued, "What are you doing here, Stella?"

"Ummm…I'm a nerd, remember?" Stella said with crossed eyes and they laughed. She could feel Ray staring at her while she had her banter with Sebastian. She looked in Ray's direction, and he looked stiff having Meghan draped over him.

"You're the hottest nerd here. Where's your boyfriend?"

Seb asked the question and Stella, knowing Seb as well as she did, knew he was trying to start trouble, or maybe he was trying to figure out why she had tensed up when he picked her up. She answered without looking at Ray. "No boyfriend. Just Kayla with me. She's over there collecting numbers and posting pictures on social media." Stella pointed and laughed. Seb's eyebrows went up, and he looked in the direction Stella was pointing.

"That's interesting. Since you are collecting numbers, take mine. We can grab a bite before we leave." Sebastian winked at her. She sent him a text message so he had her number too. To Stella, Seb was just as hot as Ray, but he wasn't Ray. Seb was a little shorter than Ray by an inch. His hair was a dirty blond; his eyes were green. He had that California look even though he was from Brooklyn and Puerto Rican too. They exchanged numbers, which she knew could be dangerous, but freak it. She gave Seb another hug and could feel Ray wanting to linger longer. Stella knew his mannerisms, and he was rocking back and forth on his heels. That usually meant he was anxious or nervous. She waved to him, said goodbye, and continued to the bathroom. As they walked away, she faintly heard Meghan say, "Finally. Jesus. Ya'll were talking forever." Stella went into a stall and let go of the breath she hadn't realized she was holding in. She heard her phone chirp. It was Sebastian sending emojis of smiley faces. Stella knew Seb had felt her tense up. She saw it in his face.

Ray pulled Sebastian so only he could hear him while Meghan was busy looking through her phone. "I have to go back," he told Sebastian. Seb nodded and winked at him.

"Meghan, look at these purses over here. Don't you love these?" Seb said dragging her attention away to the purses while Ray walked back toward the bathroom.

Chapter 7

When Stella finished using the bathroom, she came out and saw Ray standing there…alone this time. She walked up to him, and he met her halfway. The spark between them was still electric. They smiled at each other as thousands of people walked all around them. It still felt as though it was only them.

"How are you?" she asked him with knots in her stomach.

"I'm, uhhh, good. Better now than I was before," he said with a serious look on his face.

"You look good together. I hope you're happy" She didn't really hope that bitch made him happy, but it was the cordial thing to say.

"Thanks." He had his hands in his pockets, as if to keep from reaching out to touch her.

Stella looked around them and said, "Looks like we both finally made it to Comic-Con San Diego." It was something they had talked about doing while they were together.

"Yeah, I always thought we would do this together," he said with something that looked like regret in his eyes. She tried to change the subject.

"How's the voice acting coming along?" she said with a hopeful smile. His face said it all. He did not look happy.

"It's ok. I had to get a regular job to pay the bills for now. Sometimes the voice work is steady, and then other times it's dead. Sometimes I wonder if I made a mistake."

"You absolutely did not. Stop thinking that way. This has been your dream since forever. Dreams don't happen overnight." She reached out and touched his arm, more out of habit than anything. The contact from touching him sent shockwaves through Stella's body. It was a feeling she hadn't felt in four years, arousal. He looked down at her hand and took his hands out of his pockets. Did he feel it too? Whenever they had deep conversations or when she knew he was going through something, she would touch his arm and try to ease his concerns. She looked him in the eyes and said, "Just be patient. It will all work out, and before you know it, you'll be some major character on some crazy Marvel movie, and you'll be on your way!" He looked at her and smiled. She felt that electricity again where her hand lay on his forearm, and she removed it fast. Regardless of the heartbreak she felt when he left, she always believed in his talent and was positive he would make it. Stella always gave him the inspiration he needed whenever he was feeling down about his mission to become a voice actor. She meant every word she said, and she wasn't just stroking his ego.

"Thank you for the vote of confidence," Ray said, and he winked at her. They stood staring at each other. He reached out and traced her scar with his thumb. His hand caressed her face. She closed her eyes and leaned into his hand. Her heart felt as if it would explode from beating so fast. He felt so good, familiar, and she missed him so much. When she opened her eyes, he had taken a step closer to her. Looking up at him, she could see that he had the question about her scar in his eyes. She had to remind herself that he had a girlfriend now.

"I should get back to Kayla," she said clearing her throat and breaking the tension.

Ray took a step back and said, "Yeah, I should get back to Seb and Meg before Seb kills her."

He gave her a hug, and she didn't tense up. He felt…safe. "Thank you," he whispered in her ear.

"Anytime," she responded breathless from having him in such close proximity and not being able to do anything about it.

And they each walked in opposite directions. Not before looking back at each other. She knew she was in trouble. On the flip side, after being together 3 years, the look on his face told her, he was in trouble too.

When Stella got back to Kayla, Kayla looked at her as if she had three heads. "What took you so long?

I was about to send out a search party. I got worried," Kay said with a genuine look of concern.

"You wouldn't even believe it…" and Stella went on to tell Kay the story.

Chapter 8

Kayla sat there with her jaw on the floor. "It's fate. You were meant to be. What are the odds you run into him among a hundred thousand people??" Kay asked with her eyebrows raised.

"I don't know, but he has a girlfriend, and she did not look happy," Stella said with a chuckle. "Especially after the way Seb gave me a giant hug and gave me his number." Kay looked at her with raised eyebrows. The same raised eyebrows Seb had had when he heard Kayla was there too.

"She'll get over it…Sooooo how did he look? How do you feel?"

Stella closed her eyes, trying to relive their hug, and answered, "He looks great, as usual. He was wearing a regular white T-shirt, and it was clinging to his chest. He was wearing jeans and sneakers. As for how I feel…ummm, I'm not sure. I didn't take his number, so we'll probably never see each other again." Stella thought it was best at the time to delete his number so she wouldn't call or text him after he left.

"But Seb got your number, right?" Kayla asked and Stella nodded. "And that's how a wingman does it!! Good for Seb. Trust me, you'll be hearing from Ray,"

Kay said with a giggle. "Were you ok with Seb hugging you?" Kayla knew her friend well.

"I tensed up, and I think he noticed," Stella replied with a worried look. Kay nodded. "But I didn't tense up when Ray hugged me, which was odd because I know Seb is safe."

Kay thought for a second and answered, "But Seb doesn't know your body like Ray does. Your body and your mind know it. So they're just protecting you from everybody."

"They did notice my scar, and Ray touched it. I know he's going to ask."

"Well, you tell him whenever you're ready." Kay paused and asked, "How did Seb look?"

Stella smiled and wagged her eyebrows. "Girl, finer than Brooklyn."

Kayla threw her head back. "God, he's so fine. That should be considered a sin." They cracked up. "Now let's go finish enjoying these exhibits!" They stood and kept walking through the convention center. Stella wished she could focus, but all she wanted now was to be walking through this show with Kayla, Seb, and Ray. Especially Ray.

Seb drove back to the hotel with Meghan and Ray in the backseat, and he could tell Stella just changed his friend's life. Smiling to himself, he decided to have a little fun on this ride back.

"Man, Stella still looks fantastic after all these years, right? She hasn't changed one bit," he said looking in the rearview mirror at Ray's face. Ray looked back at him with a smirk and replied, "Yes she does."

"Somebody should really give that girl some lessons on how to dress. Yuck. Who wears a jersey over a tank top anymore?" Meghan chimed in rolling her eyes.

"*Tirala por la ventana, Ray. Mandala pal carajo ya,*" Sebastian said looking at Ray with a giant smile in the mirror. Ray didn't like anybody talking about Stella. It didn't matter who it was. He turned toward her with his nostrils flaring.

"Why is it any of your business what she was wearing?" he said through his teeth.

"Why are you getting so offended, Ray? Huh? You want her back? You think she's going to take you back with your broke ass? I don't think so. You're lucky you have a woman that wants you. She left you so you could have your big break that never came, stupid," Meghan yelled in his face, and then moved to the opposite side of the seat.

"*La ventana, Ray,*" Seb said with a serious face now. Ray had to close his eyes to keep his composure.

"And you keep talking your taca taca as if I don't know you're talking about me," she said directing her slander toward Seb.

"Bitch, don't come for me. I'm not Ray. I will tell you exactly how I feel in English, you fucking *pendeja coño.*"

"Enough!" Ray bellowed. They were constantly arguing, and he had a headache. These were going to be the longest four days ever.

Chapter 9

Later that day, back at the hotel, Stella was in the shower when she heard her phone chirp with a text message.

Seb: Your boy has you on the mind. Meghan is mad as hell and it's not going well, They had a blow up in the car

She closed her eyes and pinched the bridge of her nose. She hadn't come here for drama. How the hell could she have known she would run into him? Her phone pinged again.

Seb: Don't feel bad. She sucks anyway and they're no good together. I hope he can finally see it now.

That offered little consolation. She hadn't come to break up anybody's relationship. This was supposed to be an exciting getaway, which it was turning out to be in more ways than one. Stella decided to reply.

Stella: I'm not sure why she's so upset. Ray and I haven't been together in four years. Anyway, the convention is amazing!

Seb: Yes, it is. So much walking though! Hey, listen, if me hugging you made you uncomfortable, I apologize. I was just so excited to see a familiar face.

Stella felt bad. He did notice. She had never meant to tense up, but she had not been able to get over being hugged by any man. Except Ray, apparently, because she hadn't tensed up with him. It was as if her body knew.

Stella: Omg no! that was my fault. My body is just acting weird in its old age lol.

She was trying to lighten the mood.

Seb: lol

And in that moment, she knew she would have to eventually explain what had happened to her.

She dried off and finished putting her pajamas on. Kay was already in bed. They were exhausted. Between jet lag and the walking, they were ready to call it quits for the night at 7:00 p.m. Stella was exhausted too, but her mind was racing. Ray had looked sooo delicious today. She closed her eyes, and she could remember how he felt when they were together. It was intense and passsionate with three *s*'s. After what had happened two years ago, she regretted not leaving with Ray to Los Angeles. Breaking her thoughts, she felt her phone vibrate. Her heart raced when she read the message.

Ray: Hi. It's Ray. I hope it's ok. I almost beat Seb to death for your number lol.

She was going to be in for a long night. She laughed and replied.

Stella: Of course, it's fine. Lol.

He had an iPhone, so she knew he was writing.

Ray: It was good seeing you today. Seb was a little too excited for my liking but whatever.

Was he jealous?? she thought.

Stella: I was just as excited as he was.

Should she say it? Yes, fuck it. She typed out.

Stella: I hope I didn't create any problems with Meghan. She didn't look so happy

She was opening a can of worms, and she knew it. What a homewrecker, she thought to herself.

Ray: She always looks like that. Don't worry about it. How did you enjoy the convention?

They chatted for hours about the exhibits, different celebrities, shows, music. It felt like old times, and she had that stirring in her stomach that she hadn't had in a long time…since they were together.

It was midnight by the time they finished texting, and she was seeing double. Kay was in la-la land. It took Stella a while to finally drift off to sleep.

Ray kissed her neck slowly as she ran her hands up and down on his bare back. He pulled back to look into her eyes, his eyes heavy with passion and lust. He leaned down to kiss her softly. Their tongues swirled ever so slowly. They were tasting each other. Making up for four years of lost time. He picked her up and carried her to the bed. He finished undressing and positioned himself over her, kissing her slowly and moving down her neck. Moving farther down, kissing and licking her as he went. When he reached her flat stomach, he hovered there. Her body was screaming for him to move down. He looked up and smiled at her with that smile that had made her want him the first time she saw him.

He moved down and kissed the inside of her thigh. Just as he was about to kiss her core, she felt him move back up her body. Stella opened her eyes and saw Jason hovering over her.

Stella jumped up in bed with a scream. She was dripping in sweat and breathing hard. Kay groggily woke up and asked whether she was ok. "Yeah, mama, I'm ok. Go back to sleep."

Chapter 10

Ray lay in bed with Meghan next to him, and all he thought of was Stella. He always thought of Stella. Even four years later. She was always on his mind and in his dreams. He had tried to get over her after he made the decision to move out west, but there was no woman that compared to her for him. Their relationship had always been hot and heavy as they did their best to grow together when they were young. When he was offered the gig in LA, there was no way he could let it go, and he knew she would never stand in his way. It was his chance to do a show for Netflix. After seeing her today, though, he knew everything had changed. Meghan was just something to pass the time. They'd been dating for ten months. She was hot, but she was no Stella, and he had known that their relationship wouldn't last even before he saw Stella. He closed his eyes and he could remember how she felt under him, against him. He was getting hard just thinking about it. He was thinking about the way she would moan his name, the way she would tell him she loved him. The way she gave him her heart fully and unconditionally.

Those five hours they had spent texting were the best five hours he had had in four years. It was as if nothing had changed between them. She had looked so hot in those jeans and that Yankees jersey. She knew the way to a man's heart without even trying. She was a simple plain Jane. If you loved her, you loved her for her, and that was it. She wasn't trying to be who she wasn't. And she never changed.

Meghan moved, and he went still. He was not in the mood for her attitude. He knew it was ending.

He had put up with more than he should have. They had been together for almost a year, and she was verbally abusive, telling him he would never amount to anything with his job as a warehouse manager. He didn't want Stella to know how far he had fallen since he had left. He was ashamed of where he had ended up. But her encouraging words today meant everything to him. He could tell she still cared about him from the way she spoke to him, the way she looked at him, and the way she texted him. He felt alive for the first time in a long time. He thought about the text he had received from

Seb: Something is going on with Stella. She tensed up when I gave her a hug earlier and she never did that before. That scar above her eyebrow. She never had that before either.

Ray pondered what Sebastian had written. She hadn't tensed up when Ray had hugged her. At least he hadn't felt her tense up. On the contrary, he thought he had felt her melt into him, but he could have been wrong. If there was something going on with her, she would tell him eventually.

He had a tough time falling asleep after their long text conversation. He thought about their catching up on everything. Her telling him how she had moved to the city and had a dog. She had no boyfriend because she was focused on getting her own life together. He remembered all she had ever wanted was to live in the suburbs in a nice quiet house in a quiet area. Even though they were Puerto Rican, that didn't mean they didn't strive for the same things as everybody else. He was so grateful in a selfish way that she had never gotten together with anybody after him. He always knew in his heart that she belonged with him. He just wasn't sure how to make it work. All he knew for sure was that he had four days to see her and he wouldn't waste any time.

Chapter 11

Ray didn't realize he had fallen asleep until he opened his eyes and saw light peeking through his window. He went to grab his phone and realized it wasn't where he had put it. He looked across the room to see Meghan staring at him, holding his phone. Fuck! he thought.

"Do you still love her?" were the first words out of her mouth. He sat up, ready for the fight, and he really didn't care.

"Yes, I do. She was an important part of my life for three years," he said with a coolness in his voice.

Meghan stood up and threw the phone at him with all her might. Luckily, it missed him, but it hit the wall and shattered. "I'm done. You and your sorry ass can have her. I'm over this relationship that's going nowhere anyway!" she screamed. Then she turned on her heel and walked out the door with her suitcase.

He looked at the phone and shrugged. "Guess I have to get a new phone."

He went to Seb's room and told him what had happened. A slow smile spread across Seb's face. "Now you know I was never a fan of hers. You had no business being with her in the first place, and it looks to me like everything is lining up perfectly!"

Ray looked up at the ceiling and then back at Seb with an exasperated look on his face. "I need a new phone!" At this point Ray was over Meghan and happy she was out of his life. "Can you text Stel and let her know what happened?" Seb snatched his phone and hammered out a text, hit send, and put his phone back in his pocket.

"Come on. Let's get you a new phone and hit the convention. Oh my god…it's like a 120-pound weight has been lifted now that she's gone!!!" Seb said, raising his hands into the air. They both laughed. "Sooooo Stella said Kayla is with her, right?" Seb asked with his eyebrows raised. Ray nodded. "This is going to be a good time."

Stella read the text from Seb:

Seb: The witch is gone. Broke Ray's phone so he can't text. Going to get a new phone now. Will see you both at the convention.

What the hell! That had gone downhill fast. Stella sighed. They were grabbing breakfast at a diner inside the hotel—at Marina Kitchen. Kayla looked at her.

"They broke up," Stella said, and Kayla started giggling as she buttered her toast. Just then the server brought over their pancakes, french toast, and hash browns.

"Looks like this trip just got interesting!" Kayla said with a gleam in her eye. Stella was apprehensive but kept her worries to herself. "Are you going to be ok?" Kayla asked her, remembering everything Stella had gone through four years ago. Kayla had never seen her so dark and depressed. Ray was Stella's true love, and they both knew it.

Stella looked at her friend and said, "I don't know. But I guess we'll find out. I think I made the right choice four years ago, but maybe I didn't, and we lost four years of being together."

"Or maybe you guys needed this time apart to see how much you really mean to each other," Kay interjected. Stella knew she was right. It felt as if she and Ray were at a point in their lives where they were able to manage such an intense relationship. Twenty-seven felt like a perfect age to be getting their shit together.

Chapter 12

The girls got to the convention center at 9:00 a.m. It was a short walk from the hotel, which was great for them. Today felt different. There was a different energy in the air. Ray texted that he had gotten a new phone and would be at the center soon. Stella let him know they were heading for the Funko Pop booth. Stella and Kay had just made it to the booth when they bumped into two guys they had seen yesterday. They couldn't even remember their names. One was taller than Kay, with blond hair and brown eyes; the other was slightly taller than Stella, with brown hair and brown eyes. Stella and Kay kept it cordial and were trying to walk away, but these two guys were persistent and didn't want to leave. "Hey, maybe we can grab a bite to eat after the show," the shorter one said. The girls shook their heads.

"Nah, sorry, we can't," Kayla said, and she tried to keep walking.

The taller one grabbed Kayla by the arm, and Stella froze. She was getting triggered, and Kayla knew it. "Get the fuck off!" Kayla told the guy. Stella's eyes started tearing up, and she couldn't move. Kayla felt another arm around her opposite shoulder at the same time and saw a hand grab the guy by the wrist. Kayla was about to swing when she looked up and realized it was Seb. He smiled down at her.

"Is there a problem?" Seb asked, glaring at the guy and holding his wrist tight.

Kayla looked at him and smiled. "Nope. No problem here…Right?" she said, turning her head to look at the asshole with his hand on her arm. The two guys put their hands up in defeat, turned, and walked away.

Seb asked Kay whether she was ok, and she nodded. Seb had on a navy blue tank top, jeans, and Jordans. Kayla looked him up and down. She took a breath because he looked like a model. She saw Seb give her the same once-over but stopped to stare at her chest and then moved his gaze slowly up to her face. Kayla almost bit her lip but held back. He looked straight into her soul with those green eyes. "Hi, *mamita,*" he said, and he gave her a kiss on the cheek.

"Hi," Kayla said, looking at his mouth and remembering how much she had wanted to kiss those lips years ago.

Ray was at Stella's side, and he saw Stella's horrified face. He was ready for anything. But luckily those guys had walked away. "Hey, I'm right here, ma. Are you ok?" he stepped in front of her so she could see him. Stella looked at him, snapped out of it, and nodded.

"Yeah, sorry about that," Stella said, looking at Ray. Ray looked at Kay with a question in his eyes, and Kay answered back with sad eyes. They all saw Stella visibly relax next to Ray.

Ray and Seb looked at each other. Seb mouthed, "I told you."

Kayla gave Ray a hug and said, "Well, aren't you two just a sight for sore eyes!" breaking the tension. Seb whispered something in her ear, she giggled, he put his arm back around her shoulder, and they continued through the booth.

Stella was back to normal and just shook her head and looked at Ray with a smile.

"Are you ok?" she asked, referring to his breakup.

"For the first time in a long time, I really am ok," he said as they looked at each other. The real question was, was she ok? But he would ask when the time was right.

Ray saw Stella take him in. He had on a black shirt, jeans, and sneakers. She was wearing a black shirt with the Captain America logo, black jeans, and black Jordans. It looked as if they had matched on purpose.

"We look like twins," she told him, letting out a laugh.

"I swear, I did not stalk you and know what you were going to wear," he replied with a laugh.

Stella turned around and saw Seb and Kay laughing about something. They looked good together. As if they belonged together. She wandered away to stare at the wall of Pops. Could she and Ray make up for four years of lost time? What would his reaction be when she told him what had happened to her? She wasn't sure, but maybe this was divine intervention telling her yes and to give it a shot…if that was what Ray wanted too.

That was when she saw it! Stella gasped, her eyes widened and she started jumping up and down like a kid. She had been looking for it for two and a half years. Ray looked at her. "What is it?" he asked.

She walked up to it and grabbed it. "It's the only one I'm missing." She closed her eyes and hugged it. It was the original Funko of the Hound from *Game of Thrones*.

He smiled. " I didn't know you kept up with them after I left. How many do you have now?" They started the collection together.

She squinted. "With all of them…around 250." His jaw dropped. They had had about twenty when they were together.

"Don't judge me!" she said, laughing.

"Never. That's awesome. Send me pictures."

"I will. I may have some, but I have to look for them in my phone. I have no room in my apartment for them. It's so bad!" she said with a playful look. She went to the register and paid for the treasured piece. That was worth the whole trip, she thought. Well, that and this.

"Ok, sooo you want to make my mom's day?" She pulled her phone out and took a couple of selfies of herself and Ray—one of them smiling and one of her smiling and him giving her a kiss on the cheek.

She hit send to her mom after texting **Stella: Ma look who I ran into.**

Her phone was ringing before the second pic went through. She gave the phone to him. "She's going to want to talk to you. I just became second fiddle." He picked up the phone and started laughing.

"Oh, you did tell her, huh?" he said, looking at her. "I can't wait to see you either. Ok, love you too. *Bendición*. Bye."

Stella took the phone and raised it to her ear to hear her mom yelling, "*TE LO DIJE*! I told you! I knew you would see him. He looks so good, *bendito*!! You have to bring him home with you…"

Stella just listened as her mom went on and on. "Ok, Ma. Ma. Ma. Ma." She couldn't get a word in. Ray started laughing. "Ma…how's Brandy?" She listened…"Ok, good. Give her a kiss for me, and tell her I love her." She listened and said, "Ok, Ma, I gotta go. Love you too. I will. Ok. *Bendición*. Bye." She hung up. They looked at each other. "I'm never going to hear the end of this one," she said with a smile.

"I'm glad she was right!"

"Me too," she said, and they continued walking together.

Chapter 13

They all made plans that night to go out to an R&B lounge not too far from where Ray and Sebastian were staying. The girls went back to their hotel to get ready. The guys would come and get them at 7:30 p.m. While in the room, Kayla said, "Seb is going to get some tonight. I waited too many years to let this go," and she turned to Stella. "Do you think you're ready to be alone with Ray? It's obvious he's still into you and you're into him."

Stella nodded. She knew her friend was right. "I think so. Ray always makes me feel safe. Seeing that guy with his hand on your arm was a trigger, and I thought I was going to have a panic attack right there." But she had waited too long for this opportunity with Ray. He was the only one she wanted to be with. "But then Seb was there, and I thought he was going to break that dude's arm." They laughed. "Talk about coming to his woman's defense," Stella said with a raised eyebrow. "There is definitely some built-up sexual tension there."

Kay nodded. "There sure is. Who knew I had to come three thousand miles to finally snatch his ass," she said, and they laughed.

Stella looked at herself in the mirror. She had on a black dress that was a little short for her taste, but it would get his attention, which was what she wanted. She never wore dresses, so he would be taken aback.

Kay looked stunning. Her skin glowed in the light. She had on a dark blue dress. Her curves and boobs were on full display, and Seb was going to eat his little heart out. Kayla had had the hots for Seb back when Stella and Ray were together, but they had both been in relationships, so they had never had the chance to get together.

Stella knew her feet would be killing her in the shoes she was wearing and contemplated taking her sneakers with her.

At 7:30 p.m., the knock on the door came. Ne-Yo's "You Got the Body" was playing in the background. Stella and Kay opened the door together. The two jaws on the other side of the door dropped. "Ok, screw the lounge. Let's just stay here," Seb said, giving his flowers to Kay and pressing his forehead against hers. It looked as if they were ready to be alone now. They all laughed.

Ray walked slowly to Stella with a raised eyebrow and a half smile as he looked her up and down. He was getting hard just looking at her. Down boy, down, he told himself. He also had flowers for her in his hand. Peach roses since he knew those were favorite. Her heart was beating fast again like it always did when she saw him. He looked so handsome. He was wearing a dark blue button down shirt, black slacks and black dress shoes. Stella was having a hard time breathing just looking at him. She exhaled as he took her hand and brought it up to his lips. "You look beautiful," he told her almost in a whisper, and she blushed.

"Thank you. You look so handsome." Maybe Seb had a point about staying. She took the flowers from him. The girls put their flowers on their small table, grabbed their purses, and let the guys lead the way.

Ray drove, with Stella in the front seat. Seb and Kay were sitting in the back seat whispering to each other. They had rented a black Nissan Altima with leather seats. Stella kept looking at Ray as he drove. It was a big turn-on. He was so confident in everything he did. Strong, handsome, confident, handsome, strong…did she say those to herself already? But seriously, he was smart too. They arrived at the lounge at 8:00 p.m. and they could hear the music pumping. Stella loved R&B, and Ray knew it. She and Ray walked hand in hand, and it felt so good to both. Familiar. Safe. They were led to a private table.

It was Friday night, and it was getting crowded. A steady crowd of mostly African Americans and Hispanics was streaming in. There was a small dance floor with a few people on it already. The DJ was playing a variety of songs. They sat, and Ray had the server bring them a bottle of tequila. Stella was down for a few shots to take the edge off. Whenever she was in a crowd of people, she would be extra vigilant about who was in the crowd. She and Kay were already sway-ing to the beat of the music.

The server came back with the tequila, and Stella took the initiative to pour out the shots. Kay had her phone ready for their selfie. With three shots poured, they all posed for their photo and took the shots to the head. Ray had a soda since he was driving. The liquid burned Stella's throat, but it was exactly what she need-ed. Ray looked at her. She never had alcohol when they were together. "Yeah, I drink now," she said laughing. Ray laughed, but he kept replaying Stella's look of hor-ror when that guy had grabbed Kay's arm. What was going on? He would find out when Stella was ready.

Stella had started drinking after what had hap-pened to her so that she could fall asleep and almost became dependent on it. It came to a point where she had to wean herself off. Kayla was watching her closely to make sure she didn't overdo it. Stella gave her a look that said she was ok. Kayla relaxed.

Seb, Kay, and Stella each took one more shot, and "That's the Way Love Goes" by Janet Jackson started playing. Both Kay and Stella stood up, grabbed their partners, and led them to the dance floor. Stella had Ray behind her with his arms around her waist while she swayed to the music. She had her eyes closed as she enjoyed the music and the feeling of having Ray with her in this moment. She turned to face him and wrapped her arms around his neck. He pulled her closer and buried his face into her neck, and they continued dancing. She closed her eyes and felt him kiss her neck. He remembered how much she loved that. She got chills all over her body. It was surreal being with him there. He pulled back enough to look at her, his forehead resting against hers. They were both breathing hard.

He finally made the move and brought his mouth against hers slowly and softly. The sparks she had thought would be there were an understatement. There were fireworks. There were explosions.

He put his right hand on the side of her face and gave her a long, gentle kiss. This had never felt so right for both of them. He pulled back long enough to look at her. She looked up at him with heavy eyes, and she wanted to cry. She needed him. His warmth, his comfort, his love, his strength, his safety. When he had left, she had put up a wall around her heart, not letting any emotion get to her after Kay pulled her from the dark place she had gone to. And then after what she had gone through with Jason, she never wanted to see another man ever again.

Her eyes were tearing up, and he thought he knew why. He was half right. They had never spoken after he left, and he felt horrible about it. She fought those tears with everything she had. She put her head down and walked back to the table. He followed closely behind her, holding her hand.

Kay and Seb were still on the dance floor, holding each other close. It looked as if they were making up for lost time, all the years they had lusted after each other but couldn't do anything. Stella sat down and fanned herself. She took a drink of water, suddenly feeling hot.

"Are you ok?" Ray asked, looking at her.

"Yeah, I'm good. I just needed a minute. It's so hot." They sat together holding hands. They stared at each other with regret in their eyes, knowing they belonged together. Everything happens for a reason, Stella thought. It had to—otherwise Stella had gone through that trauma for nothing.

Kay and Seb came back to the table, and Kay looked at Stella with a smirk. Stella whispered in her ear, "Uh-huh…y'all gonna get some," and they both laughed. Cracking up, Stella looked at Seb, leaned in toward his ear, and said, "Thank you."

Seb looked at her and said, "You're welcome. I need my best man to be happy, and he hasn't been happy since you."

Stella nodded at him. "Me either." If it weren't for him giving Stella his number, they wouldn't be here right now. Ray knew it too. Seb was a good guy.

Kay leaned into Stella and whispered as low as she could with the music blasting, "I'm going to fuck the shit out of him later." They busted out laughing. The guys had to laugh.

Stella grabbed the menu. "Guys, I'm going to grab a bite. I'm starving."

"Should we leave?" Ray asked leaning down into her ear.

"Nooo, I love the music," Stella whined as "Missing You" by Case played in the background. Stella sang along and Ray smiled. The waiter came, and they ordered a sampler tray to share. Seb was about to sign the tab, but Stella stopped him and put her card in for half of it. They signed something before the server left. The tequila was hitting, and Stella needed food. They were all feeling nice, and Seb's green eyes were unapologetically devouring Kay, just as they had the first time they met. In Stella's mind, all she wanted to do was jump onto Ray's lap. But she wasn't sure how she would react in real life.

A waiter came back with the food, and he looked like Jason. His build and those facial features that haunted Stella every night. This guy could be his twin. Stella froze, and Kay noticed. Kay grabbed her hand to bring her back quickly. "Hey Stel, what's the name of this song again?" Ray and Seb noticed again and their brows furrowed.

Stella snapped out of it and said, "'I.F.U' by Usher." She looked at the food. She was starving.

Seb whispered in Kay's ear, "What's going on?"

Kay looked at Seb and shook her head. Seb nodded and Kay knew he understood she couldn't tell him.

They all ate, and the DJ started playing "Doin' It" by LL Cool J, and Ray knew it was about to get real. The girls jumped up. This was Stella and Kay's song.

All four headed to the dance floor together with what felt like the rest of the lounge. Everybody got up. This time they all danced together. Stella and Kay were putting on a spectacle dancing back to back. The whole lounge was singing. Stella hadn't felt so good in so long. Ray was standing in front of her, feeling the music too. This was one of those songs that brought it out of everybody. The whole lounge was singing in unison. Everybody was dancing with or without a partner.

The song ended, and everybody knew it was time to leave. Seb and Ray walked to the side to talk. After a minute or so, they came back to Stella and Kay. Seb whispered in Kay's ear, and she nodded. Ray took Stella's hand softly and brought her close so he could whisper in her ear, "I don't want to leave you tonight, and those two want to be together. Do you want to stay with me in our room?" he asked. Ray had ended up checking out of his room and moving into Seb's room since Meghan had left and he no longer needed a room to himself.

Stella hesitated for a second but then nodded. She didn't want this night to end. Kayla gave her a questioning nod, and she nodded back. It had been a long time since she had both been alone with a man and been intimate with him. At least she had made sure all her lady parts were ready for the occasion.

She knew she would be safe with Ray. It was ok, she told herself.

Chapter 14

Ray and Stella dropped Seb and Kay back at the Marriott and headed to Ray's hotel. "Have fun!!" Stella yelled at them with a laugh from the window as they walked inside.

Kay turned around and yelled back, "You too!!"

Once they were inside, Ray drove off. He looked over at Stella and she looked nervous. Ray turned in to the parking garage of his hotel fifteen minutes later. He was nervous too. He got out of the car and went to help Stella out on her side. They walked together, holding hands tightly and in silence, as they approached the elevator. This building was tall. They got into the elevator, and he pushed the button for the twenty-sixth floor. Stella tensed up. She smiled when Ray held her close on the ride up. That meant he remembered her fear of heights. They got off the elevator and walked to his room: room 2609. "I should tell Mami to play 2609 for the Win Four back home," Stella said and Ray let out a laugh.

They walked in, and Stella threw her shoes across the room. Ray knew those shoes were killing her. "I should have brought my sneakers," she said with a pout. Ray laughed. Stella looked around. The room had a beautiful view and was much larger than theirs.

It had a kitchenette, a living room space, a bathroom, and a bedroom. She walked over to the window.

The lights were dim, giving a warm ambiance to the room. "Are you thirsty?" he asked her.

"No thanks," she replied, and she noticed he had a Bluetooth speaker in the room. She quickly connected her phone and put on "For the Record" by Mariah Carey. The words to the song couldn't have been truer right then in that moment. She had always loved music, and she would move to anything. She saw his reflection behind her.

He pressed his chest against her back, and she leaned into him with her eyes closed. He put his hands on her waist and turned her to face him. She looked up at him, mouthing the words to the song. He bent down to kiss her, and the kiss turned from soft to more urgent. It was glorious feeling his tongue swirling around hers. But it had been a long time and she had been through a lot since then. Stella pulled away needing a minute. Ray looked at her.

"Stel, I know something is wrong. What happened?"

She looked at him with pleading eyes and sat on the sofa. Was she ready to tell him? Was it better for him to know right away? If he wanted to run away, she would rather have it happen now than drag this out. Her tears started falling before she started talking. Ray felt helpless and sat next to her.

She took a breath and said, "Two years ago, I went on a date," and she saw his jaw clench. This was her first time telling her story to anybody but Kayla.

"What happened, Stella?" he asked softly, holding her hand.

"He walked me home, and I had opened my door—" She had to pause because every time she thought about opening her door, it made her angry. How could she be so dumb? She knew it wasn't going any further with him. Was the door opening a sign for him to think something more would happen? "He leaned down to kiss me." She felt Ray's hand tighten on hers. "But I turned my face because I just couldn't do it." Ray audibly sighed, but he wasn't ready for what she said next. Stella put her head down, looking at their intertwined hands, and continued, "Everything changed. He got so angry and grabbed my arm hard. I tried to pull myself free, but I couldn't. He was just too strong." Ray went still as she continued, "He shoved me into the apartment, and I swung and punched him in the face, but it was like nothing. He punched me with a closed fist. That's how I got this scar." He squeezed her hand and needed to know what had happened next. "I hit the floor, and he pinned me down. He was slapping and punching me. I was trying to get free, and I just couldn't." Her tears were falling faster now. "I felt him trying to unbutton my pants, and I started kicking my legs, and he punched me in the stomach, which cracked a rib." Stella's voice was getting smaller. "I couldn't breathe, and I couldn't move." She closed her eyes. She saw it all happening so clearly in her mind. She looked Ray in the eyes when she said her next sentence so that she could see his expression. "He raped me."

Ray felt himself lose his breath. It was as if he had been physically hit by something huge. He was also hit by something worse. Guilt.

Stella continued, "When he finished, he got up and left. I couldn't stand up, so I crawled to my bag and called Kayla. She came and took me to the hospital. I told the doctors I fell down some stairs, but they didn't believe me. But if I wasn't telling them what really happened, there was nothing they could do." He held her as she cried.

"I'm so sorry" was all he could say. He was so angry in that moment but was trying to shield her from seeing it. But she knew him well and could feel it in his body language. He hated himself for leaving. If he had stayed, she never would've gone on that date. She would have been safe. She wanted to see his face, and there was so much going on. He asked the question she knew he would ask. "Did you go to the police?"

She shook her head. "No. For what? I just wanted to forget it ever happened. And what good would it do anyway? It would make him angry, and he would continue coming after me. But I did have Kay take pictures which I kept in my phone," Ray understood what she meant.

"So you have certain triggers and that's why you freeze under certain circumstances, like when Seb hugged you?" he asked. She nodded.

"Does this change anything?" she asked him, feeling defeated.

"Change what? How I feel about you? Are you crazy? I'm never letting you go again, Stella. Nobody will ever hurt you again," he told her, looking her straight into her soul. He held her until she finished crying.

Stella got up to wash her face. She knew she looked like a mess and was embarrassed. Ray still thought she was the most beautiful woman he had ever seen. Ray was stunned by what she had told him. The fact that someone had hurt her the way she was hurt made him furious. If he ever found the guy, Ray was going to jail. He knew that for a fact.

Stella came back and sat down with something that looked like relief in her eyes. "You know something, Ray—after telling you everything that I've never told anyone but Kay, I feel like all this pressure I had on me from not telling anyone was lifted. Not even Ma knows."

Ray wanted to see the pictures. "I'm glad you felt comfortable enough to share that with me. I'm sure it wasn't easy." He paused "Stel, show me the pictures."

Stella's eyebrows shot up "Oh my God, nooo," she said. He turned her to face him.

"I need to see it, Stel. Please," he pleaded.

She hesitantly got her phone, opened the folder labeled "never dating" with the pics, and handed it to Ray.

Ray didn't recognize the person in these photos. Jason had beaten her so badly that her face was all types of colors. Her body was all types of colors. Her arm where he had grabbed her was awful. When Ray finished, he gave her the phone back. He couldn't handle seeing her like that. No wonder she had tensed up when Seb gave her that big bear hug.

"No one will ever hurt you again," he said softly. It was a promise he meant to keep.

"Ray, you realize I have to go home in a few days, right? You can't be with me 24/7." Ray nodded because she was right. They had to figure something out.

Stella knew she wanted to be with him and never leave. In this moment she felt better than she had in a long time. *"Hablame Bajito"* by Abraham Mateo, 50 Cent and Austin Mahone started playing.

She stood up and took his hands, pulling him to stand with her. They danced slowly to the music. Ray was holding her tightly against him, wondering how he would protect her from three thousand miles away. She pulled back to look up at him. This night would not be wasted, she thought. She pulled him down so that she could kiss him. "I want you, Ray," she whispered against his lips.

"Are you sure?" he whispered back. "We don't have to."

"Yes. I want to," she said, her lips just inches from his. She turned around and said, "Can you undo the zipper please?" He kissed her neck, and she shivered. He wanted to take things slow and savor every moment, but his body was taking over. He unzipped her dress and pulled it down, revealing her black underwear. She turned to face him. Ray drank in the sight of her. He noticed the scar she had on her rib cage and touched it. He paused and said, "You're so beautiful, Stella."

"I've missed you," she said in a low voice, looking deep into his eyes. She started undoing the buttons of his shirt. He had a white tank top underneath, and he had gotten bigger in the arms and chest since they were together. She ran her hands down his arms slowly. He was everything she wanted, she thought. She pulled his tank over his head and kissed his chest. Stella put her hand over his heart and could feel it beating fast. He did the same, and her heart was beating hard and fast too. They needed each other so badly. She never wanted to leave his side again, but she would think about that tomorrow. She looked at him as she removed her bra and panties at the same time he removed his pants and underwear.

He picked her up and carried her to the bed. Laying her down gently, he hovered over her and asked her, "Is this ok?"

"Yes, it's perfect." And that was the truth. He kissed her neck and made his way down her body, kissing, sucking, and licking as he went. He stopped at her rib cage and dropped a kiss on it with a frown.

"You feel so good," Stella said with her hand in his hair.

"Stel, you have no idea what you're doing to me. I've missed you so much," Ray said in a low, husky voice. He was going to blow soon, but he needed to make sure she was taken care of first. He moved down in between her legs, and she was in heaven. Her eyes closed as she anticipated where he was about to reach. And when he did, she cried out. It had been so long since her lady parts were given attention that it didn't take her long to feel herself building. She was afraid to open her eyes and see another face, so she kept her eyes closed. Ray had a way with his tongue that her body just responded to immediately.

She exploded, and while she was in the throes of her orgasm, Ray positioned himself on top of her. Before gently joining their bodies, he said softly, "Open your eyes, Stel."

She opened her eyes, and thankfully, all she saw was Ray's handsome face. She smiled at him, and he smiled back. He gently entered her, and it was like an out-of-body experience for both of them. They locked hands and kissed as he slid in and out of her. It was a feeling so familiar to Stella's body. They fit as if they were puzzle pieces made for each other. Stella was about to lose it, and from the look on Ray's face, he wasn't going to last too long either. He went slowly, making every second count as if it were the last. She felt so good. Like home. Her cries were tipping him over the edge, but he wanted to hold out as long as he could. They looked into each other's eyes. Stella wrapped her arms around his neck and wanted to tell him how much she loved and missed him. But she held back from the L-word. Soon he was exploding through his own orgasm, and his body lay on top of hers before rolling to the side.

They lay there in each other's arms, staring at the ceiling. "Still like old times," he said with a smirk and raised eyebrow.

"It sure was," she said, and they both laughed. She rolled over to check her phone, and she had four text messages from Kay.

Kay: Stel are you ok?

Kay: LORDT!

Kay: THANK YA JESUS

Kay: WHEW!!!!

Stella had no choice but to start laughing and replied.

Stella: Yeah, mama, I'm good. Seb was that good huh?

Kay: Girl, he hit all my spots. Imma text you back. it's round two!

Stella: Have funnnn!!!

Stella laughed, and put her phone down. Ray was looking at her. "Your boy put it on Kay. Or should I say was about to put it on Kay again!"

Ray laughed aloud. "That's my boy!" and they both laughed. "It's about damn time. They should've been together back in Brooklyn with all that lusting after each other they did."

"Tell me about it," Stella said, rolling out of bed, and she went to the bathroom to freshen up. When she was done, she came out and realized she didn't have any clothes to sleep in. "Do you have an extra shirt I could borrow?" she asked him as he lay there staring at her body.

He got up and went to the closet. "Yesss, although I much prefer the view as it is." He handed her the shirt and gave her a kiss. He had his boxer briefs on with nothing else. Stella bit her lip. He is even more sexy now then he was, she thought. They sat together on the bed and turned the TV on, and Ray flipped through for a bit before landing on Stella's favorite old-school show, *The Golden Girls*. They snuggled, watching the show and laughing, until they both fell asleep in each other's arms.

Chapter 15

Waking up today was different from waking up yesterday, Ray thought. He had had a wonderful night just holding Stella in his arms. Falling asleep watching *The Golden Girls* was something so simple, but it meant everything to him. Stella made him feel at home, and he missed it. He hadn't realized how much he missed it until last night. The familiarity he felt was overwhelming. He really wanted LA to work, but the truth was, he was not happy.

When he and Seb had set off on this adventure, it was exciting. But here they were. Seb working as a mail sorter for Mattel and Ray slinging boxes in a warehouse. He should just face the fact that he wouldn't make it in voice acting. After four years, he was ready to hang it up and get back to the life that made him happy. One that included the people he loved. If anything, he could still pursue it: New York City was just as good as LA.

It was 6:00 a.m. Stella had only her dress from last night. He gave her a kiss on the forehead to wake her up. She groggily opened her eyes and smiled when she saw him. She closed her eyes and then opened them big and looked at Ray. "That's the first time in two years I slept without waking up screaming." She looked at him. "I wasn't screaming in my sleep, right?"

She was relieved when Ray shook his head. "We both slept like babies. We have to get ready for the show," he told her. She jumped up in the bed, realizing she had no clothes. All she had was her dress of shame from last night.

She checked her phone to see three more messages:

Kay: Stel

Kay: His mouth

Kay: That is some good dick!!!

Stella started cracking up. She typed out a quick reply:

Stella: Girl I'm about to come back to get dressed. I'll text you when I'm on my way.

While she was answering Kayla, Ray got in the shower. She took the shirt he had given her off and walked slowly to the glass shower door, opened it, and got in. She was feeling strong this morning. As if she could manage anything with Ray by her side. Watching the water pour over him was a sight. She was drooling. He stepped aside so she could go under the water, and it felt amazing. She closed her eyes and felt his hard body behind her.

They knew they were pressed for time but didn't care. Her hotel wasn't that far, and it was not as if she needed hours to get ready. Stella could get ready in minutes, which was another reason she was special to him. She needed to taste him and dropped to her knees and pleasured him the way she remembered he liked.

Ray and Stella got back to her hotel at 7:30 a.m. She had no choice but to throw on her dress from last night. She hurried to get ready, and at 8:30 a.m. they met up with Sebastian and Kayla, who had left ahead of them to get breakfast and to wait in the line.

Ray asked her whether it was ok to tell Seb what happened to her because he was worried about her and she said yes. Seb had always been like a brother to her and always looked out for her. Kay and Stella walked ahead, and Ray let Seb know what had happened.

"Kay, I feel great today. I slept without waking up screaming for the first time in two years."

Kay wrapped her arm around Stella's shoulder and said, "Some good dick will do that for you." They both started laughing.

Stella looked back, and Seb was frowning while listening. When they were done talking, Seb came and gave Stella a hug lightly this time. "I'm so sorry I grabbed you the way I did. If we find him, he's dead. You know that." Stella nodded. She didn't tense up this time.

Ray watched them, and he knew he would have to let her know what had been going on in his life over the last four years too. He was not looking forward to it and hoped she wouldn't run away from him.

Chapter 16

t was Saturday, and the best panels were today. New Marvel shows were coming down the pipeline, and the convention was showing brand-new trailers. They got to their first panel at noon. Stella looked at Kay, who was looking adoringly at Seb. Stella smiled to herself. She hadn't seen her friend look so happy in a long time. Not even when she was with Jack. Breaking her train of thought about how happy Kay looked, Ray grabbed her hand. She looked at him and smiled. The panel was starting.

A gentleman who looked to be in his midforties sat next to Ray. He looked familiar, but Ray couldn't place him.

The panel started, and questions about the show were asked and answered. The exclusive trailer they were waiting for played. Stella held Ray's hand tighter while watching in awe. Ray looked at her, wondering how he would let her go in a matter of days. He turned his attention back to the screen. When it was over, a round of applause broke out.

The panel was over, and they stood up to leave. Ray decided to break out his Marvin the Martian voice. "Mmm at last. That was earth shattering!"

Stella always loved when he did that voice and started laughing.

The man next to Ray turned to him and asked, "You do voices?"

Ray replied with a guarded "Yeah."

The man stood about five foot seven and weighed around 150 pounds. He wore glasses and had salt-and-pepper hair. "I'm Vincent Flemming. I'm a talent agent and would love to see what you can do." Vincent gave Ray his card.

That was why he looked so familiar. Vincent Flemming was a huge talent agent for his own company, the Flemming Agency.

Ray was stunned. "Ray Garcia. Yes, I'm familiar with the talent you work with." They shook hands.

"Come to my office in LA Wednesday morning at 9:00 a.m. so we can discuss opportunities," Vincent told Ray. That would work, since Ray had to go back to LA anyway.

"Looking forward to it," Ray responded, still at a loss for words. Vincent walked away.

He felt Stella next to him. She was giddy after the interaction. "Holy shit!" she said. "That was huge!" He looked at her with a big smile.

"It's about freakin' time!" Seb said behind Stella. Ray did not want to get his hopes up. He had done so before only to get his heart crushed when it didn't work out.

"This is the break you've been waiting for. It's your time," Stella said with genuine excitement in her eyes for him. This meant he couldn't look any further than Wednesday. He and Stella looked at each other. All he saw staring back at him was someone who wanted him to be happy, even if that meant letting him go again. Well, today was Saturday. They were all leaving on Monday. So they had today and tomorrow. He would make the most of it.

Stella and Kay went to use the bathroom.

Seb looked at him and could tell his mind was turning and said, "You came out here for this." Ray knew his friend could tell how he was feeling. Seb continued, "Things are different now. We're older now. I think you can figure out how to make the long-distance thing work. Anybody that knows you both knows how much you love each other. It's obvious, and after what happened to her, there's no way I'm letting you let her go again. She needs you, and you need her."

Ray let Seb's words sink in, and he nodded his head. He had never stopped loving Stella, and now that he had her back, he didn't want to lose her again. The question was how to make it work.

"It's going to be ok," Kay told Stella while they were in the bathroom.

Stella was so happy for Ray. This was his big break. She was excited for him. Inside she knew what this meant. They would continue to be apart. Her heart broke just thinking about it. She was going to just enjoy the next two days and see what happened. She smiled at Kayla. "Yeah, it will be. I just want him to be happy."

"You make him happy. He makes you happy. The way you two look at each other, you were meant to be. It'll all work itself out." Stella nodded.

"What about you and Seb??" Stella asked, wagging her eyebrows.

Kayla laughed. "It's just a fun time. He's so funny, and the sex is *whoa*." They both laughed. "Who knows what will happen?" Kay said. "You and Ray need alone time today and tomorrow so you can figure out what you want to do. Seb and I can stay in our room, and you should enjoy Ray in their room."

"Yeah, maybe. Let's see what their plans are for today and tomorrow," Stella said, reapplying her lip gloss. They walked out of the bathroom to where Ray and Seb were waiting. They noticed how women were looking at them, but as Stella and Kay were walking toward them, the guys only had eyes for them.

Ray's eyes were expressing something that Stella had seen before, four years ago. She knew he was already questioning himself about what to do. "Stel, do you want to stay with me today and tomorrow?" he asked her.

She grabbed his hand. "Yeah, I think that sounds like a plan."

They all went back to their hotels—Stella to grab her things and Seb to grab his stuff so they could switch.

"Are you sure you're ok with this?" Stella asked Kay.

"Absolutely. I need my bestie to figure out what's next with the love of her life. You have not been happy since he left. And from the looks of it, he wasn't having any luck with love either. Seb said that Meghan bitch was a nightmare. If there's any chance that you can be together, go for it. Life is short, and I need nieces and nephews." They laughed. Stella gave Kay a hug.

Chapter 17

Stella got dressed up for dinner and had her bag set by the door when there was a knock at 7:30 p.m. She opened the door, and the guys were standing there, Seb with his bag in his hand.

"Come on in," she said. They walked in, and Ray gave her a kiss, their lips lingering for a touch longer than a hello. "You look amazing," he whispered to her.

"Thank you," she said, blushing. "So do you," she said, looking him up and down. His white polo, jeans and boots looked so hot on him. Jesus, Stella thought.

"Yup. My *motetes*," she said, and he laughed.

"I haven't heard that word in a long time," he said with a smile. It was Spanish slang for things or belongings.

They said their goodbyes to Seb and Kay. Ray left them with the keys to the car, and they took an Uber to drop off her things at Ray's hotel. From there, they headed to a restaurant called Born and Raised. They were seated outside with a view of the city. It was a stunning restaurant.

They sat across from each other and each ordered a steak. She didn't want to look like an animal, but she was starving.

This place was pricey. "We're splitting this bill," Stella told him without breaking eye contact with the menu. "There's no way I'm comfortable with you paying for this whole meal." Since he wasn't driving tonight, he decided to indulge and ordered two shots of liquid courage. One for her and one for him. Ray was a person of few words, but he wanted to make sure Stella knew how much she meant to him.

The shots arrived. They clinked glasses. "To new beginnings!" she said with a smile.

"To new beginnings," he responded. They took the shots, and the alcohol burned on the way down. Fortified with the liquid courage, he grabbed her hands. They looked at each other. "Stella, you know I'm not good with words, but I need you to know how I feel." She looked at him, listening intently. He blew out a breath. "Leaving you the first time was the hardest thing I ever had to do. We were young, and getting that call to come to LA was everything I thought I wanted. You were so unselfish in the way you encouraged my dream, and I was so lucky to have you. I know I hurt you when I left, and I'm so sorry." Her eyes were glistening; the memories of how she had felt four years ago when he left were fresh. "I never thought I would ever have a second chance with you. I figured you were married with kids by now. But here you are. Single. Here with me." He paused for a beat and continued: "I don't want to lose you again. You've made me realize how much I miss you, how much I miss home. These last few days have been the best days since Brooklyn. Obviously, I have this meeting on Wednesday that could change my life, or it could be nothing. Regardless, the only thing I need or want is you back in my life, not only as my partner but also because I want to make sure no one can hurt you ever again. Can we figure out how to make this work?" He rushed the words out.

She was ready to respond. She stood up and went to sit next to him on the bench so that she could be close to him when she said what she had to say. Hooray for liquid courage. "Ray, I've loved you for seven years. Just because we weren't together doesn't mean you haven't been a part of me for the past four years. I could never give my heart, my body, my soul to anybody the way I gave them to you." The thought of Jason taking a part of that away from her made her angry. The thought of what she had gone through made Ray feel ill. She continued, "This trip that I never thought I would ever take has turned into a dream. Having you here with me has changed me. We are both older now. I think if we put our heads together, we can figure out how to make this work."

He touched his forehead to hers. "I love you too," he whispered, and he gave her a kiss. He still had more to say, but at that moment, their food came. Their eyes opened wide when they saw the portions they were served.

"Who the hell is going to eat all this???" Stella said, and they laughed. They ate as much as possible. It was delicious. When the check came, she grabbed it, and he grabbed her hand. "Nope. Don't even play with me," she said, and he knew she was not laughing. He pulled out his wallet and she pulled out her wallet. If he was going to splurge, he was happy it was with her. When the waiter came back for the check, she handed it to him with both of their cards.

The food was amazing, and the evening was amazing, but all they wanted was to be alone together. His hand rested on her leg. Four years ago, Stella had never worn dresses. Seeing her dressed like this was a huge turn-on, and she knew he liked what he saw. "Can't wait to get back to the room," she whispered teasingly in his ear.

"Are you sure?" he replied. "I don't think you're ready for all this," he said, pointing to himself. They both laughed. He was so funny. Stella had missed that—just having somebody to laugh with. The cards came back, and they signed their receipts and headed to catch an Uber.

In the Uber, Stella checked her phone quickly. She had a message from her mother.

Sandra: How's my son-in-law? read the text message. Stella rolled her eyes.

"Mami wants to know how her son-in-law is doing."

"Tell her that I said I'm good," Ray said with a laugh. Stella tapped out the reply and threw the phone into her bag.

She rested her head on Ray's shoulder, enjoying the ride in silence with him. Holding his hand tightly, not wanting these two days to end. He rested his head on hers. He closed his eyes and sighed.

Chapter 18

They arrived at the hotel room, and Ray led her inside. Turndown service had already passed. The lights were already dimmed, the bed made, the room cleaned. Ray walked over to the bottle of tequila and poured two shots. He gave her one and said softly, "To us."

She replied, "To us."

They put the glasses down. Stella walked into his arms and wrapped her arms around his waist. He wrapped his strong arms around her and closed his eyes, holding her tight and close to him. They were inhaling each other. Dreaming of the life they wanted together.

Stella stepped back with a mischievous grin on her face. She pushed Ray back until he sat on the sofa. She connected her phone to the Bluetooth speaker and let the liquid courage course through her body. She put Lite FM 106.7 from New York on. It was their favorite station. "Don't Wanna Lose You" by Gloria Estefan was playing.

Ray's eyes bored into her as she began sliding the straps of her dress down her shoulders. She turned around and finished bringing the dress down her body slowly. She turned again to face him and loved watching his face as she walked over to him in her bra and underwear. He grabbed her hips and kissed her stomach. Stella grabbed his head and pulled him closer to her. Ray pulled her down until she was straddling him. She could feel how turned on he was and proceeded to lift his shirt over his head. She kissed his neck while he unfastened her bra. Once it was off, his mouth went to work on one nipple while he grabbed the other. She moaned. She had never thought she would feel this way again, but in the back of her mind, she had known there was only one person who could make her feel like this. Nobody else. She started grinding on his hard shaft and heard him moan while he was sucking. She was soaking wet and needed his pants off.

She moved off him, knelt in front of him, unbuttoned his pants, and pulled them down, along with his underwear. She grabbed him, and he shivered under her touch. Stella leaned down to lick him and looked up at him when she put him in her mouth. He threw his head back, and his hand went to the back of her head. Feeling her mouth around him was amazing. She always knew just what to do to make it feel amazing. The way she stroked him had him ready to explode.

Stella got up, removed her panties, and sat on his swollen manhood. They both let out moans as he filled her. "Oh god Stella," he said as he felt her. The need to have him inside her was too much. She started moving up and down. They kissed passionately without breaking stride. "I love you, Ray" she said, out of breath.

Ray held her hips tight to slow her down. His hands coming up to her face and looking deeply into her eyes. Hearing the words he'd dreamt of while making love to Stella was almost more than he could handle. "I love you more," he said, straining to hold himself. They kissed and she started moving again. He didn't want this to end. Ray wrapped his arms around Stella and could tell she was about to go over the edge and wanted to make sure they did it together. Her eyes squeezed shut, and her moaning got louder. As soon as she came, Ray came with her. They sat there just holding each other.

"I'm not moving. Nope. You can't make me!" Stella said laughing.

Ray was stroking her back. His mind was racing. He didn't want her to move; he wanted her there always and forever. She was the only woman that he had said the L-word to and meant it. He loved her so much.

"Hey, do you want to skip the convention tomorrow?" he asked. She looked up at him. "I know the tickets were expensive, but to be honest I just want to spend time with you," he said, stroking her hair.

So did she. "Sounds good to me," she said with a smile. She finally moved off him and went to the bathroom with her things. When she came out, Ray had on his boxer briefs, and all she could think of was round two.

She grabbed her phone and had three text messages.
Kay: How's it going?

Kay: Hello

Kay: OH, **it's going that well.**

Stella: Kay idk how I'm going to leave him. I don't know what to do.

She hit send and put the phone away, not realizing she was frowning just thinking about what she had written.

"Everything ok?" he asked.

She turned her frown upside down and said, "Yes, everything is perfect."

Chapter 19

Stella let Kay know that they wouldn't be going to the convention the next day. Waking up with Ray was surreal. She woke up first and watched him sleep. He looked so peaceful and relaxed. She couldn't help herself as she reached up and gently touched his face. He didn't move. She loved him so much it hurt. "I should have just come with you four years ago," she whispered. They would've been married and had kids or been close by now. She looked over at the clock, and it was 7:37 a.m. Since they had nothing to do, she nestled closer to his body, her back against his chest, and closed her eyes. Ray shifted and held her tighter against him, and she could feel him getting aroused. He would never get enough of this either. He kissed her neck and started round three from the night before.

They finally got out of bed at around 11:00 a.m. Today they were going to find a Latin restaurant. Since she didn't have a proper kitchen and couldn't cook for him, the least they could do was find a place to eat. It was her treat today because she wasn't comfortable with him paying for everything. Today was dress-down day, and they were just going to enjoy each other.

They were ravenous by the time they arrived at the Puerto Rican restaurant *Jibaritos de la Isla*. Ray walked in and stopped. He closed his eyes and inhaled. "I haven't had real Puerto Rican food in four years," he said with a smile. The decor was very homey—Puerto Rican flags everywhere, things for sale from the island, a backdrop for taking pictures.

They sat, and Stella noticed the waitress giving eyes to Ray, who was oblivious. Yes, he was fine. And he was hers. The end. She laughed to herself. They gave the waitress their order—since they wanted to try different things, they ordered *arroz con gandules* (yellow rice and pigeon peas), *pernil* (roast pork), chicken stew, *chicharrones* (fried pork), *maduros* (sweet plantains), and empanadas. The waitress gave one last, long glance in Ray's direction, and Stella rolled her eyes. "What happened?" Ray asked, looking around.

"You have an admirer," she replied with another roll of the eyes.

Ray laughed. "Jealous?"

Stella smirked. "Nope. You should give her your number." And she rolled her eyes again. They both laughed.

Stella saw a couple of guys sitting in the path of the bathroom. Her jeans were extra tight, and her curves were on full display.

"I have to use the bathroom. Be right back." She got up slowly and gave her hips an extra sway as she walked past the two guys and headed toward the bathroom. Both guys gawked as she passed. Ray watched and muttered "Touché, woman" under his breath. He didn't like it one bit, the way those guys looked at her ass. Stella came back five minutes later, and in her peripheral vision she could see the guys watching her go by, and her eyes locked on Ray.

"Well played," he said as she sat down.

She laughed. "Whatever do you mean??" she said, feigning innocence. Ray didn't like to admit he was a jealous person, but Stella knew how to get him worked up.

"So let's talk about how to make this work," he said, taking her hand.

"Well, there's social media, which I don't think is conducive to a relationship," Stella started. "But we have FaceTime and text."

He nodded. "Yeah, and we can take turns flying back and forth to see each other."

"Absolutely," she agreed, and she continued, "I have to see how much longer I have on my lease." She thought for a bit. "I think it's like three months or something."

Three months sounded like forever. "Well, let's see what happens on Wednesday first," he told her. Their food came, and they ate, enjoying themselves. Salsa was playing in the background. Ray ate as if he hadn't eaten in four years.

"How come you never came home to visit?" she asked him while putting a fork full of rice in her mouth. It was a question she had always asked herself. As much as her mother loved Ray, Ray's mother, Maria, loved Stella. Sandra and Maria were friends and stayed in touch, so Stella would've known if Ray was back.

"Because if I had gone back, it would have been to see you. I didn't want to rock the boat in case you had moved on with your life," he said, chewing, his face serious. "I wouldn't have been able to see you with someone else." She understood how he felt. Seeing him with Meghan had almost ripped her heart out. "Once I have that meeting on Wednesday, I'm booking a trip to New York. It's time for me to come back." Stella looked at him with excitement in her eyes. The thought of having him home was the most comforting feeling she'd had in a long time.

"Your mom will be super excited to have her baby home. Hell, my mom will be super excited to have her baby home." They both laughed.

They left the restaurant and walked aimlessly, hand in hand. The weather was beautiful— seventy-six degrees with a warm breeze. They stopped at a pond and sat on a bench. Ray turned her toward him. "Are you going to miss me?" he asked while moving a strand of hair from her face.

"I already do," she said with a pout. And then her face got serious.

"What are you thinking?" he asked her.

"That I'm a moron and should have just gone with you when I had the chance four years ago. Would've saved us all this heartache."

"Stel, you did the right thing. You gave me the space I didn't even know I needed at the time. It would've been so hard on us both, coming out here, and I think you would have resented me after a while. It was difficult at the beginning not knowing anybody but Seb. Missing you, missing my family, missing Brooklyn. I struggled a lot when I first got here until I got into a rhythm. Even now, working at that warehouse is so demotivating for me. I did not want you to see me working that job." There was more he needed to say, but she interjected.

"First of all, you know it's not just a job. You are doing what you must do to survive. Don't ever think it is beneath you to be working that job. There are hard-working people working right alongside you, trying to make a better life for themselves. Our people, blacks, browns, Asians, immigrants, all kinds of people going through shit that we can't even imagine. If you don't want to work there, use it as motivation to strive for what you want. I'm so glad you had Seb with you to ease all the adjustments you went through out here. I can't even begin to imagine what you felt."

He absorbed what she had said. She was right. He wasn't better than anyone. He had spent the past three and a half years feeling sorry for himself. She could tell he was thinking about what she had said. He just had a new appreciation for his job and his coworkers. He had been so busy pitying himself when he should have realized that he was more fortunate than most. This was why he loved her.

"Tomorrow, you go back to LA, and I go back to New York. At least I can see you on FaceTime, and we can text, until we see each other. We got this," she said, and she showed him she was strong by flexing her arm. They laughed. He did his Popeye voice. She loved it.

Just then her phone chirped. She looked at the message

Kay: Do we have to leave?

Stella: Unfortunately, yeah. Are you catchin' feelings???

Stella had not seen this coming.

Kay: I think so. This is so out of character for me, but he makes me feel so different. Alive. Sexy.

Stella:. I know. Like I told Ray, at least we have FaceTime and text

Kay: It's not enough

And that was the problem they were all facing. It wasn't enough.

Stella looked at Ray. "Looks like Kay and Seb are having the same long-distance dilemma we are."

"Great. Now we can all cry together," he said jokingly. They got up and continued their walk.

"What time is your flight tomorrow?" she asked him.

He pulled out his phone to check the ticket. "Um, looks like the flight is at 3:30 p.m. Boarding starts at 2:50 p.m. Which means I have to be there by around oneish. What about yours?"

"My flight is at 2:00 p.m. Boarding starts at 1:25 p.m. I land at freaking 11:00 p.m. almost," she said, rolling her eyes. That time difference was crazy.

"How did you deal with the flight?" He knew she was petrified of heights.

"Ummm, badly," she said laughing.

"You needed me there to hold you," he said, looking down at her.

"Yeah, I did!" she exclaimed. "Oh my God, the turbulence felt never ending. I was shitting in my pants."

He busted out laughing. "At least my flight is only one hour."

"Yeah, yeah, keep bragging." She poked him. Their relationship had always been easy. They went with the flow, and whatever came, they dealt with it.

"Do you remember when we first met?" he asked her. Of course she did. She smiled. Those memories were still in her phone.

"I sure do. I still have the pictures from that day."

He looked at her with wide eyes. "Do you really? I lost them somewhere in the cloud. Can you send them to me when you have a chance?"

Stella stopped at a bench and sat. She opened her phone and started scrolling for the pictures. She found them. July 25, 2015. There was one of them smiling on Coney Island Beach with the sun setting behind them.

Chapter 20

July 25, 2015—Stella and Kay were in Coney Island just enjoying themselves. At the time Kay was dating a guy named Jack, who was with them. Stella was the third wheel. While Kay and Jack got on rides together, Stella went to the arcade to play the basketball game she loved. One game opened, and someone was playing next to it. She stepped up to the game, slid the card, and looked up and to her right. Ray was there and staring down at her. He was so fine, she thought. But guys like him were not interested in her. He smiled, and she smiled back, not thinking anything of it. Turning her attention to the game. It started, the balls rolling down, and she started doing her thing. Making shot after shot after shot. Ray stood there watching her. By the time the game ended, she had almost sixty points, and there was a crowd watching.

"Hold up. You were cheating, right?" Ray said to her.

She laughed. "Absolutely not—they were all net. Weren't you watching??"

Sebastian was there and stood next to Ray. "Dude, those were all net," he said laughing. He had his arm around some girl whose name Stella couldn't remember.

"Wanna play against me?" Ray asked, his eyes bright with excitement.

"Sure, let's do it," she said with a big smile. And they went head to head. At the end, the score was 55 to 50 with Stella winning. Ray couldn't believe it. He had never seen anybody that good, and he loved that game.

She turned to him and said, "Good game," giving him a high five. He held on to her hand for a beat. She felt a spark but dismissed it. Stella turned to walk away from the game, but Ray continued talking.

"Um, hey…my name is Ray," he said, sticking his hand out.

"Stella," she replied, shaking his hand. Yes. Definitely a spark.

"How did you learn how to play like that?"

"Well, first I love basketball, and second I love that game, and to be honest, it's the perfect distance for someone my height," she said with a scrunched-up face.

"CHEATER!" he exclaimed, and they laughed. "Would you mind if I walked with you? I'm kind of a third wheel. That is, if you're not here with somebody," he said, praying she was alone.

"That's funny. I'm a third wheel too. That's why I was in the arcade. My BFF is with her boyfriend." Stella looked around and then looked him up and down and finally said, "Yeah, sure. You don't look crazy to me, and I'm a fairly good judge of character," she said, looking at him sideways.

"I promise I'm not crazy," he said, smiling at her. Stella had no idea who this guy was, but she was feeling things she had never felt before. Her stomach was in knots. "Do you like these rides?" he asked her, gesturing toward all the rides.

"Yeah. I used to come here when I was young with my father. He used to love coming out here. Nathan's was his spot," she remembered fondly. He looked at her thoughtfully. He didn't want to pry.

She realized what she had said. "Oh my god, you just met me, and I'm telling you about my father." She slapped her forehead.

"Nah, it's ok. I asked about the rides."

"The short answer is yes!" she said, mortified. She felt like an idiot.

"Come on—let's go get on the Cyclone! And tell me more about your dad," he said.

"Let's do it!" she responded, and they headed for the rickety old wooden coaster. While they were walking, Ray told her he was from Brooklyn and he and his mother lived in an apartment near Bushwick. She told him she had grown up in the Gowanus projects but now she and her mother lived in an apartment in Cobble Hill—rent regulated, so they got lucky amid all the gentrification. She also mentioned her dad had passed away a couple of years ago. Ray empathized. His dad wasn't in the picture, so his mom had basically raised him on her own.

They were both first-generation Puerto Ricans born in New York City. Their parents, born in Puerto Rico, had had dreams of succeeding in the land of opportunity. Stella's dad had worked in a warehouse up until he got sick, and her mom had been a stay-at-home parent. She was always at Stella's school whenever Stella got awards or was playing basketball for the school team. Both of Stella's parents were dark and spoke fluent Spanish. Stella looked like a white girl and spoke broken Spanish even though her parents spoke only in Spanish. Go figure. The struggle of the Nuyorican. Not all. Most were lucky that the language came out naturally. Whenever they took pictures, it looked as if Stella were adopted. But Puerto Ricans came in all different colors, from white to dark dark. Stella's maternal grandmother was dark, and her paternal grandmother was white. Hence Stella's complexion.

Ray's dad was a traveling musician that couldn't keep it in his pants from what his mom told him. There were no pictures of him anywhere since Maria didn't want to be reminded of him. She had to work as a secretary to make ends meet for them. It was a constant struggle, but she never gave up. Ray was her reason for living. He looked just like her and was just like her. Well, he tried to be. His Spanish was a little better than Stella's, since his mother had forced him to speak it to her. and it worked in his favor. He was bilingual, smart, handsome, funny. All the girls wanted him, and he had just ignored them until now. He didn't want to be like his father, and his mother was so proud of the way he treated her and any woman he came across.

This woman he had just met was different. She wasn't trying to hit on him or get into his pants, which intrigued him. They reached the ride. He paid for his ticket, and she paid for her own ticket, even though he offered to pay for hers. She didn't know him well enough to let him pay for anything.

She typed out a quick text to Kay to let her know where she was and who she was with. They got on the ride. In the front row. He looked over at her as the ride ascended and said with a big grin, "Are you going to grab on to me when it drops?"

"No way!" she said with her own grin. Little did he know Stella was terrified of heights but loved getting on roller coasters. So yeah, she probably was going to grab him.

"Yeah, you are. Uh-oh, here we go," he said, and he screamed when the ride started to drop. Stella laughed and screamed and had no choice but to grab his arm. He felt so good. They had a vibe. Whatever this was, something was happening between them, and she didn't know what. He grabbed her hand as the ride roared and they screamed. She had never had a real boyfriend before to know what this feeling was.

When the ride stopped, he got out first and grabbed her hand to help her out. That was so much fun, she thought. They stopped to see the picture of the first drop, and there she was, holding on to him for dear life with a big smile on her face, and him with a bigger smile.

"What a great picture," she said quietly.

"Yeah, it is," he replied. Stella saw him staring at her. She had her hair up in her signature ponytail and was wearing a tight-fitted Marvel T-shirt, tight jeans, and Jordan sneakers.

"I mean, I might as well get a copy just to remember the time I met a complete stranger and got on rides with him," she said, and she stepped up to the booth to get the eight-by-ten photo and keychain.

He was in awe of this person he had just met. She was funny, naturally beautiful (since she didn't look as if she had makeup on), liked Marvel, as he could tell from her T-shirt, and smelled and felt amazing. She played basketball like nobody's business. She couldn't be real.

Stella carried the bag with the pic and gave him the keychain. "If you want to remember some random chick you met in Coney Island."

He took the keychain and put it on his keys. "Trust me, I'm never forgetting you," he said with a serious face.

Stella looked at her phone and had a text

Kay: Who is he?

Stella: Girlllll. Idk but he is fine and a nice guy! I think I'm just gonna wing this and see where it goes. Don't worry. He's not crazy. Go have fun with Jack. I'll find my way home.

Kay: Are you sure?
Stella: Yeah, I'm sure

She sent the text and put her phone away. It looked as if Ray was texting away too.

"I told Kay to just go about her business with her man. I don't want to intrude on their privacy."

"That's exactly what I was telling my friend Sebastian."

They walked and got on more rides together. Stella was enjoying herself, telling this stranger things about her life. She was working as a cashier at a local C-Town supermarket for the time being and helping her mom with the bills. He was working delivering soda to bodegas. Also helping his mom with the bills. He told her he was a year older than she was and that he aspired to be a voice actor. He loved doing voices.

Then they heard music coming from the boardwalk and walked toward it. There was a crowd forming. There was a band playing salsa.

"Do you dance?" he asked her, motioning toward the other partners on the floor.

She was shy. "Yeah, I do. Do you?"

He nodded. "You wanna dance?" He looked at her and wagged his eyebrows up and down.

What the hell, she thought. He took her hand and led her to where the other partners were dancing. Ray just wanted an excuse to hold her as much as possible. They started moving, and Stella smiled when she saw he really could dance, and she let herself go. He spun her to see whether she could keep up, and she did. He smiled and said, "Weppppaaa!" She laughed. The song finished, and everybody was hyped. The band was good. Ray felt his heart beating fast even after they finished dancing.

"You're really good," he said as they walked away.

"So are you!" she said with a smile. He was a little too perfect.

"Sooo is there anything you can't do?" he asked. In her mind she thought, yes, there's one thing. She never had a real boyfriend to do other things before but she would keep that to herself. She shrugged. He took her hand, and she didn't pull away.

They found themselves sitting on the beach at sunset. It was the most beautiful sunset she had ever seen, here with this stranger who was making her feel things. She pulled her phone out, and they turned to take a selfie. They took one smiling. And then she felt his lips against her cheek. They looked really good together. After the picture, they turned back to face the sun and the water.

"This is beautiful," he whispered. He grabbed her hand, and they sat as close as they could to each other. There must have been something in the air, because Ray was never so forward with women, but here he was. He needed to kiss her. He looked down at her the same moment she looked at him. He leaned over and kissed her lips softly. Her heart almost exploded. She had kissed guys before, but they never felt like that.

"Wow," she heard herself whisper. He moved forward again and kissed her a little more urgently this time.

He pulled away. "Stella, I normally never talk to girls and kiss them when I meet them." He said quickly. "There's something about you that has me captivated." She knew what he meant. Was this what love at first sight was? She didn't know, but if she hadn't believed in it before, she believed in it now. It existed right here, right now in this moment. She reached up to touch his face. He was so handsome. He closed his eyes and pushed his head against her hand.

The sun finished setting, and they got up reluctantly to leave. Holding hands, they walked back to the boardwalk. What a day.

Chapter 21

Stella and Ray smiled at each other, coming back to present day, recalling the memory fondly. "It was the day I realized love at first sight truly existed. I loved you from that day on, and I never stopped," she said.

"Me either. It was perfect. I floated home on cloud nine and wanted to scream from the rooftops that night," Ray said with a crooked smile. "It was the best day I spent with a girl up until that point. My heart was fluttering from the moment I saw you. I was so proud of myself for not letting you just walk away from the basketball game. That sunset was everything to me." He said looking at the picture fondly.

"Me too," she said, and they continued their walk.

They had to pack their things, so they headed back to Ray's hotel to get Stella's bag. She had to head back to her own hotel to pack the rest of her things.

Kayla and Seb were back in the room after spending the day together roaming around San Diego. Kayla sat on the bed, and Seb took his shirt off and sat next to her. In only his tank top. Kayla was ready to jump his bones again. She couldn't get enough.

"Kay, I know I wanted you back in the day, but I'm feeling something more happening here between us," he said looking her in the eyes.

Kayla nodded her head yes because she felt it too. "Yeah, I definitely feel it too, Seb."

"What are we going to do about it?" he asked running his fingers up and down her arm.

"I'm not sure, but let's just enjoy each other tonight," she said in a whisper. He nodded seriously as he moved in to kiss her. The way he kissed her made her feel like the only woman in the world. Jack had never made her feel like this. Seb's green eyes mesmerized her. He knew how to use them when he needed to. Kay felt herself falling hard, and there was nothing she could do about it.

It was about 5:00 p.m. by the time Stella got back to the hotel. Seb met Ray downstairs when he dropped Stella off. Stella gave Seb a quick kiss on the cheek and ran upstairs. Kayla was in the room, sitting on her bed. She looked at Stella, and Stella knew that face all too well. Stella went and sat next to her. "This trip has been something else," Kay started. "I came out here to have a good time, and I ended up falling in love. How does this happen? Is this how it felt when you fell for Ray?"

Stella nodded. "It was explosive. You just feel it. It's crazy. You feel it throughout your whole body."

"I knew I wanted to have a fling with him 'cause he's just too fine. But I never expected any of this. And I think he feels the same way. We've had so much fun these past two days, and it was just because we were trying to give you and Ray the space you needed after all these years. Jack never made me feel like this. Not even the first time we met. Seb and those friggin' green eyes always hypnotizing people, and that body," Kay said with an eye roll, and she threw herself back on the bed.

"Well, I can vouch that Seb is a good guy with a good heart, and nothing would make me happier than seeing you together. You look like you belong together. Girl, he is getting better and better with age," Stella said, and she let out a whistle. "Ray and I were reminiscing about how we met in Coney Island and how it was love at first sight. I mean, it had to be because there's no other explanation for what we felt that day. We spent the day together as complete strangers and ended up in a three-year relationship. All I know for sure is that I'm not losing him again. I have to go back home and figure all this out. Do I want to move to LA? I really don't know. I would have to take this godawful flight again to LA and see what his life looks like. Where he goes shopping. What the people are like. Will they accept me and my Brooklyn-ass accent? Not that I care, but I don't want to move out here, hate it, and then resent him for it. It's not fair to him. As for you, this is the honeymoon phase. You haven't really dated enough yet to make any big decisions about moving anywhere, but all I can say is to follow your heart, 'cause your heart is going to tell you what to do anyway, whether you like it or not."

Kay was listening intently. "You're right. How could I make any decisions when for all intents and purposes Seb and I are strangers emotionally? Definitely not physically, 'cause the good Lord knows!" They giggled. "Once I'm back home and we start really talking without the physical, I'll know fast whether he and I are a good match. Physically, we are compatible. I'm upset he was dating that ditz all those years ago."

"It just means it wasn't the right time yet," Stella said and her phone chirped.

Ray: I miss you

And there was a picture of Ray with a sad face in the passenger seat of the Altima.

Stella: I miss you more. Can't wait to see you tonight

Chapter 22

The four of them had plans to meet up at 8:00 p.m. for dinner and a Latin club.

"Let's make them eat their hearts out for the final night," Kay said.

The girls were dressed super risqué when it was time to leave. Kay was dressed in a low-cut short black dress with super high heels. The deep V-neck showed off her boobs the way she wanted. Her makeup was on fire. She had her hair up in a messy bun. Stella had on a dark blue dress. The V-neck was also super low, and the dress was short as hell. She kept pulling it down, wishing some more material would grow. She left her hair loose, which was very out of character. "I feel like a tramp," she told Kayla, who laughed aloud.

"Good! It's one night to help hold your man over until he sees you again who knows when." She was right. Stella needed Ray to remember this night for a long time. But she was worried about the attention she would bring to herself after trying not to bring any attention at all for two years. Seeing Ray's face when he saw her would be worth it, though.

The girls left at 7:45 p.m., hoping to make a grand entrance for the guys. Stella texted Ray to tell him they were on the way to the restaurant. Ray replied that they were almost there and would be waiting for them to get out of the cab. As they were approaching, they saw the guys waiting for them. "I'm nervous," Stella said.

"Me too," Kay said, but she didn't look it. "Let's get their ass." Kayla got out first, and Seb's eyes opened wide when he saw her. Ray watched Stella get out of the car, and he walked in front of her to take her hand.

"Wow," he whispered as he kissed her. She smiled up at him. He looked her up and down. "You look stunning. Do you feel ok?" He knew her well.

"Yeah, I'm ok. I have to make sure you are satisfied since I won't be seeing you for who knows how many weeks or months," she replied as they walked into the restaurant.

"You did an excellent job. I cannot wait to get back to the hotel tonight." He said it with lust in his eyes. He stared at her barely covered ass and bit his lip.

They sat, and he saw all the waiters looking at Kay and Stel. They looked amazing. He and Seb looked at each other like "holy crap."

"Yo, Stel, you look crazy with that dress—in a good way. Kay, you finally rubbed off on her," Seb said to Stella.

Kay brushed her shoulder off. "It took a lot to get her to buy the damn dress."

Ray winked at Stella. "So happy you got it." He said and Stella smiled coyly. She told him what she wanted so he could order for her, and Kay did the same with Seb. Ray put his hand on Stella's leg, and she looked at him. He was hard and she wasn't even doing anything.

When the waiter came, he took their orders and walked away, but not before looking at Kay's V-neck. Seb noticed and was about to stand up, but Kay held him down. Seb was upset, and it took a lot to get him mad. Kay whispered in his ear, and he calmed down.

Stella wasn't comfortable with all the attention. She just wanted Ray's attention. Ray knew that. But it wouldn't stop men from staring. It was driving him crazy, but he was trying to keep his cool. He looked at her and imagined what was underneath, and the thought drove him crazy too. Should they go to the club? He wasn't sure, but he was sure he wanted to be with Stella. He whispered in her ear, "Are you sure you want to go to the club?" She nodded.

"Why? Do you want to do something else?" She looked at him with wide-open eyes. Not even talking about that. But he laughed.

"Obviously, I wanna do something else. But I just want to enjoy my time with you." She knew what he meant.

"No, it's ok. We can go to the club for a bit," Stella said. Just then the waiter brought the shots, and Seb watched him as he dropped them off and kept going. Whew, they all thought. Seb wasn't the type for confrontation, but he was protective of Kay. They all saw it. Ray had never seen this side of Seb. Not even with other girls. That meant Kay was important to him.

They lifted their shots. Seb looked at Kayla and said, "To our last night." They all said "to our last night" and took the shots. Since the guys had taken a cab, Ray could have a shot or two tonight. He wanted to be as relaxed as possible with Stella in that dress, knowing she would be getting the wrong attention.

Chapter 23

They arrived at the club at around 10:00 p.m. The music was thumping. "La Gozadera" by Gente de Zona and Marc Anthony was playing. Couples were on the dance floor grinding. They went to the bar, and this time they could feel eyes on them. It had Ray and Seb both with their Spidey senses up.

"I do not feel good about this today. I think we should go before some shit pops off. Seb is already on the edge, and I know Ray has a temper," Stella told Kay in her ear.

Kayla agreed. "Let's just dance to one song and bounce."

Stella leaned in toward Ray's ear and told him, "One song and we leave. I know you're not comfortable, and neither am I." Ray nodded. Seb heard her and nodded too. They looked military with the faces they had on. Stella felt bad. The DJ started playing *"Yo Naci En Puerto Rico"* by Angel Canales. She and Kay went to the dance floor with the guys. Ray had his hands tightly on her hips. She could feel his tension. That was the Brooklyn in her. He was stiff, and Stella could feel him. She had to loosen him up. She put her arms around his neck and forced him to look at her.

Kay did the same with Seb. The music took over. Ray was a hell of a dancer, and so was Stella.

Ray and Stella locked eyes, and soon she felt him relax as he dipped his head down to kiss her. They were salsa coordinated, and at one point, when Ray turned her, she saw Kay and Seb were killing it themselves. Soon they were the only couples dancing, and everybody was watching them, singing and clapping. It was a beautiful thing when Hispanics and all Caribbean ethnicities got together. They were a proud people.

When the song finished, Stella was out of breath, and she had to use the bathroom. She could not hold it. She told Ray, and his face had worry all over it. It was just the bathroom, she said, and she showed him where it was in case there were any problems. She grabbed Kayla, and they started walking to the bathroom. They could feel eyes on them but got there fast, used it, and came out quickly. There were two guys standing outside the bathroom. Big guys. Bigger than Seb and Ray. Kayla grabbed Stella's hand and tried to go by them. Stella heard the biggest guy there yell with a slur "mami!" but she kept going with Kayla. He obviously had too much to drink. He grabbed Stella's arm hard. Stella froze. Kayla felt her stop and looked back. Stella could not move. Kayla grabbed her other arm and tried to yank her away, and suddenly Stella was in a tug-of-war between this drunk ogre and Kayla, who was strong in her own right. Before she knew what was happening, Ray was in front of her, shoving the ogre, who finally let go. Stella snapped out of it just in time to see the ogre swing at Ray, who dodged and cocked back and swung himself, connecting with the ogre's jaw.

Stella heard the crack and heard Seb yell, "Run!" The last thing Stella saw was the ogre falling and Seb standing in front of the other guy to make sure he did not interfere. All of a sudden, there was a stampede. They needed to get the hell out of there fast. Kayla grabbed Stella and saw the guys right behind them.

Once outside, Stella looked at her arm, which was turning all kinds of colors. She was easy to bruise, and the way the ogre had grabbed her, she knew it would leave a mark. The spot where Kay had grabbed her other arm would bruise too.

"Let's get the fuck outta here," Seb said, breathing hard.

Stella was looking at Ray's hand, which was getting swollen, and Ray was looking at the nasty mark already on her arm, and he was angry. Kayla got the Uber to get them out of there. Once in the car, they all calmed down.

"Are you ok?" Stella whispered to Ray.

"I'm fine," he said in a growl. "Are you ok?" He softened immediately, touching her arm.

"Yeah, I'm fine. No big deal." Then he saw her other arm and looked at her. "Kayla was tugging me away from him." She shrugged. "I'm ok," she reassured him. "Should've just held my pee, but I was gonna go right there on the floor." It was silent for a second, and then they all laughed.

"That big dude thought he could out-tug me. Fuck outta here," Kayla said.

Stella laughed. "Nah, he wasn't winning that. My arm almost came out of the socket." Kayla and Stella laughed. The guys were not amused.

"You could have been hurt," Seb and Ray both said at the same time. The girls felt bad. They were right. That could have turned ugly if they hadn't left. Ray had this pain behind his eyes. Stella looked at him.

"I'm ok," she said. He nodded.

She heard Kayla telling Seb the same thing. She had never seen either Kay nor Seb so vulnerable.

The Uber dropped Kayla and Seb off first. Kayla and Stella were going to meet early at their room.

Chapter 24

Stella and Ray were quiet on the ride back to the room. When they got out, Ray had her hand tightly in his, and he led the way to his room. She followed quietly. As soon as they got into the room, Ray turned, and pulled her tightly against him. His mouth crashed down on hers. The way his tongue was moving against hers, she could feel his urgency. He leaned back and looked at her. "You don't understand how worried I was about you."

"I'm ok," she reassured him. He touched her bruises. He was so angry because he could not protect her as much as he wanted. "Ray…I live in New York. You won't be with me 24/7. I've survived the last four years alone." He knew she was right, but if he was around, nobody would ever touch her again. Seeing that big guy with his hand wrapped around her arm and the look of horror on her face had sent him into a rage he hadn't felt in a long time.

He pinned her against the wall and held her hands up over her head. "Is this ok?" he asked her, and she nodded. She felt him pulling her skirt up and she closed her eyes. He released her hands and dropped to one knee, his hands pulling her underwear down. She could hear him moan as he kissed her inner thigh.

Stella put her hand in his hair and whimpered as she felt him lick her core. "Oh god, Ray," she choked out. His tongue was teasing her and driving her to the brink of madness. Standing up, Ray pressed his forehead against hers and kissed her gently. She could taste herself all over his lips.

"Mmm. You taste so good ma," He moaned against her lips. She slowly unbuttoned his pants and started bringing his pants down. He picked her up, and she wrapped her legs around him. He sank into her, and the feeling was overwhelming. His eyes rolled to the back of his head. "*Ay dios mio* Stella," he said gruffly in her ear. "You feel so fucking good." The emotion of the night was carrying them into bliss, and they both moaned loudly. Crying out his name, Stella was in ec-stasy as he pounded into her against the wall. She didn't want him to stop. Clinging to him for dear life, she felt herself tensing up and knew she was about to explode around him. "Cum with me, ma," he whispered in her ear. She came hard around him and she felt him tense up as well and slow down. He moved them both to the floor gently. He looked into her eyes. "I love you more than anything, my Stella." She put her hands on either side of his face and kissed him softly.

"I love you more than anything, my Ray," she said, and, in that moment, she knew what she wanted. It didn't matter where they lived as long as they were to-gether. Her priorities had shifted in a matter of hours.

They lay on the floor, Stella's head on his shoulder. She grabbed his right hand and noticed it was swollen. She jumped up, put her robe on, and went to get ice. When she came back, Ray was sitting on the sofa.

Stella wrapped the ice in a napkin, sat next to him, took his hand, and put the ice on it. They sat in silence. He turned and looked at her arm, where the bruise was more visible now. The sight of her being hurt in any way was a new feeling to Ray. He was seething and couldn't let it go. He had nearly blacked out when he saw that guy grab her. Both he and Seb had jumped in so quickly, and he threw the punch without a second thought. It had been a long time since his Brooklyn had come out. He laid down with his head on her lap while she continued putting the ice on his hand. She leaned forward and kissed his forehead.

"Ray," she started. "If it's ok with you, I would like to move to LA with you," she said softly. He looked up at her with big eyes. "I know I have to get a job, and we can figure out living arrangements once I have a clear vision in my mind after I get back to New York and do research. But I need to be with you. Mami is a grown woman and can take care of herself. By the way, she's dating some guy who seems nice, so maybe it's time for me to give her some space. The only person I will miss is Kay. But I think she'll be visiting LA too now, since she and Seb are together. There is really nothing holding me back from doing whatever I want. I'm sure my boss will give me a great reference, and I can get a job here at a law firm or something. I can support your dream however you need while being with you. Not to mention that I know I'll be safe here."

"Stella, that means everything to me. Having you here would change my whole life. Let's see what happens on Wednesday. If something pops off with this Vincent, then we can make the plans to have you and your dog, Brandy come out here. If nothing happens, I think it's time for me to come home," he said, looking at her face for a reaction to what he had said. Her eyes opened wide.

"Why would you come home?"

"Stella, New York is my home. You're my home. I miss my mom. I miss your mom. This actor life is hard. I don't know if this is what I want anymore."

"This is all you've ever wanted. You're about to get your big break. It's coming, Ray. Maybe the last four years were just prepping you. You remember everything happens for a reason, right? I believe something amazing is going to happen on Wednesday." She had always pushed him to better himself. She had always found him gigs when he lived back home. Stella wanted ed whatever was going to make him happy. He just nodded.

This night had taken more of an emotional toll than they expected. She leaned her head back on the sofa, and he sat up. She still had her dress half on.

She stood up and took it off. In just her bra now, she walked over to the garbage. She was never wearing that thing again. She didn't want to see it ever again. When she turned around from the garbage, Ray was standing behind her, which startled her, and she almost fell over the garbage can. He caught her, and they started laughing. He picked her up and carried her to the bed, where they could enjoy their last night together until who knew when.

Chapter 25

Kayla went into the shower as soon as they got back to the hotel. She was under the water with her eyes closed when she felt a breeze. She opened her eyes, and Seb was standing in front of her. His eyes were smoldering as he stared at her. She wrapped her arms around his neck, and he pushed her up against the wall. Kayla moaned as he kissed her neck. Seb pulled back and stared at her as the water rained on them.

"Kay, I'm in love with you. I know it's only been a few days, but I remember how I felt before I left even though I was with someone else," he said softly.

"I'm in love with you too, Seb," she said in a whisper. This was the most romantic moment of their lives. Seb wanted her on the bed for the last night. They got out and dried off. Kayla lay on the bed, and Seb crawled toward her as if he was stalking his prey. They made passionate love, making sure they knew how much they meant to each other. Caught up in the moment, Seb didn't grab protection, and Kayla didn't care. She felt so good without anything between them. Her eyes rolled back, her body feeling all of him.

"Kay," he said in a growl.

"Oh God, Seb," she cried. They erupted at the same time, and it was the most intense experience for both of them. They were sweating and in love and had no idea how they would move forward from here.

Chapter 26

At 6:00 a.m., Stella and Ray woke up. They moved about and got their things together. Since Seb was with Kay, he brought his things to Kay's room the day before. They were all going to the airport together and thankfully were all in the same terminal. Stella didn't really have anything to wear. Ray gave her one of his white T-shirts. It was going to have to be a walk of shame. She didn't want to put that dress back on. She looked at herself in the mirror, shook her head, and went to the garbage to fish the dress out. She put the dress back on and put the white shirt over it. There! That was better. Ray smiled to himself.

"What made you wear that dress?" he asked, knowing it was so out of character for her.

"Well, there was this guy, and I was trying to make him eat his heart out. And what had happened was, it was a bad idea," she finished, and they both laughed softly.

"You looked really beautiful, by the way," he said to her from across the room.

She smiled shyly and said, "Thanks."

They were ready to go by 8:00 a.m. Stella texted Kay to let her know they were on their way. She didn't want to walk in on Seb's naked ass.

They arrived back at the Marriott. Stella and Kay hugged. Seb and Ray gave each other a fist bump. It was quiet. All the unspoken had been spoken, and there was nothing else to say. They all had their bags with them. Stella looked around the room one last time. She had changed her clothes to the more appropriate jeans, Ray's shirt, and Jordans.

"Let's blow this joint," Seb said, and they all left the room.

Waiting at the gate was torture. It was time for the girls to get on their plane, and it was the hardest thing since Ray had left. They started calling the groups. They were group three. Stella hugged Ray, and he hugged her back tightly. They didn't want to let each other go. They kissed each other as if it were their last kiss. "I love you so much, Ray," Stella said with tears streaming down her face.

"I love you more, Stel," he said, feeling as if his heart were a thousand pounds.

Kay and Seb kissed and hugged. Their foreheads pressed together, and Seb touched Kay's face. "I love you, Kay. You're taking my heart with you," he said.

"I love you too, Sebastian," she said with a tear rolling down her face, and they kissed one last time before they pulled away from each other.

"Group three is now boarding."

Stella didn't want to let Ray go. But she had to. They held hands as she pulled away to get on the plane. Her heart tore. She and Kay had their tickets scanned and looked back at their loves one last time. Kay grabbed Stella's hand and pulled her toward the plane. The last thing Stella saw was Ray kissing his two fingers and sending them toward her.

Kay and Stella sat on the plane with tears running down their faces.

"Oh my God, Kay, I can't handle this feeling. It's like my heart has been ripped out again."

Stella checked her phone, and she had a text from Ray.

Ray: My love. Please don't cry. We'll be together soon. Just know that I love you more than anything.

Stella: Ray, it feels like my heart has been ripped out again. It's like when you left the first time. But worse. I love you. Have a safe flight. You'll get to LA first so please text me when you land

Kay was tapping too, probably to Seb.

Ray: I will text as soon as I land. Text me as soon as you land. I love you, my queen, my everything. You are always mine and I'm always yours. Be safe, my moon and stars

She read his words repeatedly. His reference to *Game of Thrones* made her smile. The cabin door closed. **I love you** was the last text she sent him, and then she put her phone on airplane mode. She hugged Kay, who was having her own dramatic episode from leaving Seb. They needed alcohol badly. They were sitting in first class and reached out to the flight attendant to get alcohol ASAP. The plane took off, and the tears flowed from both. This would be a long six and a half hours. The drinks came, and they drank until they had numbed the pain.

They landed at almost 10:00 p.m. Stella texted Ray that they had landed, and she had messages from him already

Ray: Hey ma we landed. I'm headed home. Missing you like crazy.

Ray: I'm home my love. Hope to hear from you soon.

He responded to her message about landing.

Ray: Oh thank God. Finally. Let me know when you get your luggage.

Kay was tapping her phone too. Stella looked at her. They were both semidrunk. The drinks had had to keep coming to get them through the flight. Kay and Stella held hands and walked off the flight. They waited for their bags and summoned a cab. The cab dropped Kay off first and then Stella in Manhattan. She would pick up Brandy tomorrow after work in Brooklyn.

She sat on her sofa and started a group chat with Ray, Seb, and Kay.

Stella: Fam, I just walked in. Love you all

Ray: Ok good.

Separately she received another message from him

Ray: Love you too.

Everything felt empty now. This was exactly the reason she hadn't let herself pine for him over the last four years. She jumped into the shower, washed quickly, got out, put her pajamas on, and hopped into bed. It was almost 1:00 a.m. by the time she got into bed. She fell into a fitful sleep and dreamed about Ray all night. And Jason's face came back into her dreams. Just when she thought she had gotten over it, she hadn't. It was probably because she had felt safe with Ray, and he wasn't there with her.

Chapter 27

Wednesday came, and Ray was nervous. He wasn't sure how to dress, so he put on a white button-down shirt, black slacks, and black dress shoes. Stella had given him some words of encouragement, but his nerves were going crazy. He just wanted to nail this. He arrived at Flemming Agency at 8:30 a.m., trying to compose himself. He wasn't going to go up until 8:45 a.m. He just wanted to settle his nerves. At 8:45 a.m. he went upstairs. The receptionist looked at him with a raised eyebrow. "Ray Garcia?" she asked.

He smiled. "Yes." Homegirl seemed like she was ready to throw her panties at him from her desk.

She smiled back. "Ok. Mr. Flemming will be with you in a bit. He's just finishing a call."

Ray sat down to wait. At precisely 9:00 a.m., the receptionist stood up and said, "Mr. Flemming will see you now. Please follow me." Ray's nerves were on one hundred.

He walked in and shook hands with Vincent.

"Ray, thanks so much for meeting with me on such short notice. It just so happens that there's a role Disney is trying to fill, and when I heard your Marvin the Martian impression, I thought you would be perfect for it. Do you do any other impressions or voices?"

And here was where Ray felt the most comfortable. "Yeah, of course," he said, and he went into his various impressions.

Vincent smiled. "Yup. Just as I thought. You're perfect. Tell me a little bit about yourself." Ray went on to tell him how he was from Brooklyn and had come to LA four years ago for an opportunity that turned out to be less than fruitful. Vincent advised him about how difficult this business was and told him to keep his head up.

"I'm going to email you a contract for using our services. There's no money that needs to be paid up front. Only if you land a gig, and then we would get ten percent of whatever you make," Vincent explained. Ray knew all this. Ten percent was standard in the industry. He was super excited. "Once you send us back the contract, I'm sending you out immediately. Your voice is special, and I think we're going to do big things," Vincent said, and he stood up, with Ray following. They shook hands.

"Thanks so much for taking the time to meet with me."

"Pleasure was all mine," Vincent said, and he walked Ray to the door. Ray wrote down his email address and details on a slip of paper and handed it to him. "You'll have that email over soon."

This receptionist was giving Ray big eyes now. Trying to be sexy. Ray wasn't having it. His woman was in New York, and she was all he wanted.

"Hey Myra…please send Mr. Garcia the contract. Here's his email address," Vincent said, handing her the slip.

"Thanks, Myra," Ray said, and he walked to the elevator.

He hit FaceTime on Stella's number. Her face popped up on his screen as he stepped out of the elevator. "I got a contract, and he wants to send me out as soon as I sign it!" he said enthusiastically. This was the most excited he'd been since he first arrived in LA.

Stella's face lit up on the screen. "I would scream, but I'm in the office!" she said with a giant smile. "Oh my God, I'm so excited for you. You know what this means, right?"

Yes, he knew. "Hurry up and get your beautiful ass out here," he said laughing. She giggled quietly. Ray saw her attention go to someone behind the phone.

She turned her attention back to Ray. "Babe, I gotta go, but I'm gonna call you as soon as I get a chance. Congratulations. This is fantastic!! Can't wait until we can celebrate. Love you."

"Love you too, ma. We'll talk later," he said, and he ended the call. He tapped out a quick text to Seb telling him everything. Now that his nerves were back to normal, he went to get breakfast at a diner and sat down to read the email.

He started going through the contract. Everything looked ok. It was a straightforward contract. He needed to get home so he could print it, sign it, and scan it back to Flemming's office. He took the day off, calling out sick so he could focus on more important things. Stella was back in his life. He had a new agent. Everything was on the up and up. Ray felt genuinely happy. There was only one thing nagging him, and it was that he had never found the right moment to tell Stella what he needed to tell her. It was something he needed to tell her face to face. And she had left before he was able to find the right time.

He got home and opened the email again. This time he noticed that under Myra's signature was her cell phone number. In the email, she had written that he could call her anytime. Yeah right. She was trying it. Ray printed the contract, read it one more time, and was satisfied that he could sign it. He signed it and typed out a quick email, making sure to keep his words professional:

Myra,
Thanks for the contract. Please find signed copy attached. Looking forward to working with
Mr. Flemming.
Thanks
Ray

He attached the contract and hit send. Within five minutes he received a text from Vincent himself with an address, date, and time. It was for an audition that day at 2:00 p.m. He replied to Vincent telling him he got it and would be there. Vincent replied, "Check your email for the audition brief and be ready." Ray got the brief, and he had three hours to be ready. The script was simple. He texted Stella quickly to let her know he had gotten the audition and would be getting ready in case she didn't hear from him.

Ray arrived at 1:45 p.m. He was as ready as he would ever be. The waiting room was packed with actors. He checked in and sat down. He read his text.

Stella: I'm so proud of you. Go kick their asses!

He smiled. It was that support that he had been missing all these years.

Stella waited anxiously to hear back from Ray. She was getting ready to leave work while Ray was at the audition. She wanted it so badly for him. Ray was strong, but she could tell he was struggling with the direction of his life. She didn't want him second-guessing himself. This was what he was meant to do and at around 6:30 p.m., she heard her phone ping.

Ray: I got it! 💪 💪

She started screaming and replied.

Stella: Ok so I'm screaming. Call me whenever you have a chance.

Ray: Ma I'll give you a call as soon as I get home in about 20 mins.

Chapter 28

Well, now Stella had to think about her next move. She had a nice nest egg saved, but would it be enough to make such a big move across the country? She was looking at apartments in LA and there was no way they could afford that, so she started looking for something with a maximum thirty-minute commute. There were some areas that had promise, but she wanted to see them first before making any judgments.

When she went to pick up Brandy the day before, she told her mother her plans and Sandra had been so excited. Sandra told Stella that all she wanted was for her to live her life. To be free and to love with all her heart. Sandra had known from the moment she saw Ray and Stella together that they were meant to be. He was a genuinely good kid, and his mom was great too. She had raised a good man. Because Stella was a tomboy, Sandra wasn't sure whether Stella would ever fall in love, but one chance encounter in Coney Island had changed her daughter's life, and Sandra was so happy for her. It broke her heart when Ray left. Stella would go into her room and not come out for hours. Kayla would have to come and pry her out of the room.

"Stella, go to LA and be with your man. Live your lives. Bring me grandbabies. Go have fun. Have an adventure you can tell your children. *Vete*. As much as I'm going to miss you, I want you to be happy more, and I know Ray is your happiness. He's like the air you breathe. You can't function without him. You've been going through the motions these past four years, but you haven't really been living."

And Stella hated that. She didn't want to admit her mother was right. Ray was everything to her. But first she had to tell her mother what had happened to her. She told her everything else but had never uttered a word about that night. As far as her mother knew, it was just a date and that was that.

"Ma, sit. I need to tell you something."

Sandra sat with an eyebrow up. "You're pregnant!"

"No, Ma. That's not it. This is not easy for me, but I feel like I must tell you to continue getting better." Sandra's face was all worry now. "Remember that date I had a couple of years ago?"

Sandra nodded. "Yeah, his name was Jeff or something."

"Yes, his name was Jason." Stella closed her eyes and inhaled. "The date didn't end the way I told you it did." Sandra faced her and listened as she went on. "He beat and raped me when he took me home." Stella stopped talking. Looking at her mother's expression made her tears start coming down.

Sandra put both hands on either side of Stella's face. "Ay, *Dios mio*, that's why I didn't see you for weeks after!" She put the pieces together. "Did you go to the cops?" Stella shook her head no. Sandra's tears were falling now because she felt as if she had failed to protect her only daughter. Sandra hugged Stella. "I'm so sorry. Does Kay know?" Stella nodded. "Of course she does. She helps you get through everything. Did you tell Ray?"

"Yes, Ma, he knows." Stella took her phone out and pulled up the pictures to show her mother.

Sandra looked. "Is that what he did to you???"

"Yeah." Sandra couldn't believe what she was looking at. Stella was unrecognizable in those pictures.

"*Dios mio*, Stella!! What did he do to you??" Sandra was trying not to be dramatic, but those pictures themselves were dramatic. She had to compose herself to be strong for Stella. "Ok. Is there anything I can do?"

"Nah, Ma. You've gotten me this far. It's time for me to take it the rest of the way and see what happens."

Chapter 29

Stella made an Excel file of everything she needed to do. She still had two months on her lease and couldn't break it before then. But she would try. What was the worst that could happen? They would say no, and she would have to wait it out for two months. Two long months. She had to figure out how much it would cost to get all her things to LA. Most of the items were Pops. She would just leave the furniture in the apartment since there was no reason to take it. That meant all she had to pack were her Pops, clothes, and knick-knacks. She would start throwing all the clutter out to get ready.

It was 7:05 p.m. when Ray FaceTimed her. She was cooking and had the phone set on her counter. "Hi, my love," he said. He was wearing a tank top, and Stella almost moaned just looking at him through this phone.

"Hi, handsome. Congratulations!! I'm so happy and excited for you."

"I can't believe this is all happening. I walked into the audition room and read the script, and they loved it. It's a Disney movie, and I'll be voicing one of the main characters. You're my lucky charm," he said with a smile.

"That was all you. I'm so proud of you. What are you going to do about your job?" she asked.

"Well, I'm going to give them two weeks tomorrow. The film starts in four weeks. So I'll have two weeks to get ready. What's new over there?"

"Ok, that sounds like a plan. I was going through all my stuff, and I still have two months on my lease, which sucks, but it gives me some time to save a bit more for the move. I'm just going to leave this furniture here since I got it at the thrift shop anyway."

He nodded. "Yes, that sounds like a plan. Less to move." He noticed Stella's arms. She had a cutoff T-shirt and was moving around her kitchen. "Your arms," he said through clenched teeth.

She looked at them and shrugged. "Yeah, it is what it is. I get bruised so easily. If I hit my knee, forget it—I have that bruise for weeks. These are gonna be there a while. It's ok. Thank goodness it's cold in the office I work in so I can wear long sleeves in the middle of July."

He needed to change the subject. "Whatcha cooking tonight?" She moved the phone to show him the salmon she was about to put in the oven.

"Tonight, we have a gourmet salmon with salt and pepper together with asparagus. I'm watching my figure again."

"You don't need to," he said. Brandy started barking.

"Brandy, come see your new daddy, mama," she said, and she sat on the floor so Ray could see Brandy.

"I'm so jealous of that dog. She looks so sweet."

"She is. I can't wait for you to meet her."

What she didn't know was that Ray had plans to come to New York in two weeks. He was leaving the day after his last day at work so he could be with Stella and his family and then use the last week before filming started to study and get his mind right. He planned on surprising her, and he couldn't wait.

Chapter 30

The next two weeks felt like forever. It was Friday, and Stella was dying to get home to Brandy and her normal FaceTime with Ray. He was working on things today, so they couldn't text, but they always spoke every night. It was 4:55 p.m., and she was getting ready to leave work. She clocked out at 5:00 p.m. and walked to the elevator with her coworker Marisol. She stepped out of the elevator and saw Ray standing outside the glass doors. She thought she was seeing things, so she wiped her eyes dramatically and looked again. There he was wearing a Knicks jersey, jeans and sneakers. A giant smile came across her face and she had to refrain from screaming. He had on a black hat and sunglasses. Jesus. Thank you for bringing this fine ass man into my life, Stella thought. He took off his hat and glasses and had a big smile on his face. She said bye to Mari and ran to Ray. They kissed, hugged, and kissed again.

"What are you doing here?" she said, almost screaming.

He laughed. "Well, I had this planned. Four weeks worked out perfect. Two weeks' notice, one week to be with you, and one week to prepare for filming." She didn't care. She was so happy he was there. "I called your mom and got the address for this place."

Just then Stella looked behind Ray's arm and saw a figure across the street that looked like Jason, but it was gone the next second. She closed her eyes and shook her head. She must be going crazy. Ray looked at her and then behind him.

"You ok?" he asked, frowning.

"Yeah, I just thought I saw something. But it was nothing," she said with a smile. Stella knew if she told Ray what she thought she saw, it would ruin this beautiful surprise. That was why she told him nothing. They started walking hand in hand. Her office building was on Forty-Eighth Street and Eighth Avenue. Her apartment building was on Sixtieth and Fifth Avenue.

On a nice day like today, she would walk home. So they walked. She couldn't believe he was there. They got to her apartment, and Brandy was going nuts. She weighed ten pounds. Ray picked her up, and she gave him all the kisses. Ray loved dogs as much as Stella did, so he fell in love with Brandy immediately. He put her down and looked around.

"Welcome to my humble home. It's not much, but it's ours," she said, a little embarrassed and feeling as though it was too small for the three of them.

"It's perfect," he said, taking her into his arms and giving her the kiss he had been dying to give her since he saw her. They pulled away from each other, and Stella looked at him.

"Oh my God, you must be starving!" she said, and she ran to the kitchen. She didn't eat out much, but she needed to feed him before they did anything. She put on a pot of white rice and prepared some chicken wings to fry. "I wish I could make you something more elaborate, but I didn't know."

"It's fine," he said, and he looked at her Pop collection. "Oh my God, you got the Golden Girls Pops!!" he said, and he started laughing.

She looked at him staring at her collection while she busied herself in the kitchen preparing the rice and seasoning the chicken with sazón and adobo. "Yes, and I got those gremlins too," she said, pointing at the female gremlin from the movie and Gizmo.

Stella had an amazing view from her window. Ray walked over to look out. "Are you sure you want to leave this?" he asked.

"Without a second thought," she said, looking at him. "You know I've always said I hate city life. It's been nice 'cause I work nearby, but I'm ready for the next chapter." She thought for a second. "Did Seb come with you?" she asked.

"Nah, he couldn't. He really wanted to. He's really hung up on Kayla."

"Yeah, so is she. That's why I asked." Stella was worried about Kay missing Seb. Normally they chatted every day, but lately they would go every other day or so. Stella needed to be there for her the way Kayla had been there for her when Ray left. Stella continued, "Their being apart is almost as bad as it was for me when you left. I think they really love each other."

Stella sent her a text.

Stella: Hey, mama. You'll never guess who surprised me at work. But I'm gonna stop by tomorrow to see how you are.

She looked at Ray and asked him, "Did you see your mom yet?"

He shook his head no and replied, "Nah, I went straight to your job to get you."

"Ok, so you go to your mom's tomorrow, and I have to go check on Kayla. I haven't heard from her, and it's not like her. I have to go see what's going on."

Ray looked concerned. He thought of Kayla like a sister the same way he thought of Seb like a brother. "Should we go check on her tonight?"

Just then Stella's phone pinged.

Kay: Ok mama I'll see you tomorrow. Tell Ray I said hi.

Stella shook her head. "No. Tomorrow is fine."

They ate and sat down to watch a movie while they digested their food. Brandy made her way on top of Ray's lap. "What a tramp!" Stella said, looking at this little dog trying to make the moves on Ray. He even had that effect on dogs, apparently, not just women. "Just throwing herself at the first man to walk through that door." They laughed. This was nice, she thought. It felt very…domestic. She felt very comfortable having him there in her apartment with Brandy next to them.

Chapter 31

Ray couldn't believe Stella hadn't been with any-body for four years besides what had happened to her, but he was so thankful. He started reminiscing. "Babe, you remember our first time together?"

Stella blushed. "Of course I do."

They had met in July 2015, and their first time happened for Stella's twenty-first birthday on November 22, 2015.

Ray knew she was inexperienced but didn't realize she was a virgin until she told him after they started dating. He let her make the decision when she was ready. He didn't want to push her, but he could not wait to have her with him in that intimate way. He rented a room in Manhattan for the night. He wanted to make sure it was memorable for her. She was special, and it was important to him that she knew how special she was.

They got back to the hotel, and the lights were low. He took his time with her body and let her explore his body in a way she was timid about. She felt so good. They were at it for two hours before he finally entered her body; he wanted to make sure he didn't hurt her. As he started sliding in and out of her, at first, he felt resistance, and then her body gave way to him, and she let out a soft cry. He stopped and looked at her. "Are you ok?" he asked.

She nodded. "Yes. I'm ok," she said, and smiled up at him. He kissed her and slowly started moving again. She had never felt anything more intimate in her life. Not that she had much experience, but still. She needed him to know how she felt. It was the first time she looked him in the eyes and said, "I love you." He responded by slowing down and kissing her. Moving her hair out of her face and telling her he loved her too. He made love to her slowly and gently.

Stella was so glad she had waited to give her virginity to someone she loved wholeheartedly and not to just anybody to get it over with. Ray treated her so special that night. When Ray's orgasm hit, he went stiff and had his head lying against her neck. He lifted his head and told her she should use the bathroom to clean up since she would be bleeding. She took his advice and went. Sure enough he was right. She put her underwear on and went back out to lie down with Ray.

Chapter 32

Coming back to the present, Stella said, "That was a special night. Fun as hell." She laughed. Brandy was sound asleep. And Stella noticed Ray's eyes growing heavy. He must've had a long day.

"Babe, let's go lie down in the room so you can get some rest," she whispered. He nodded. Standing up, he took his clothes off, and lay down on Stella's bed. He looked exhausted. Stella smiled at just having him there with her like that. She made sure he was comfortable and then went to finish cleaning the kitchen.

It was 10:00 p.m. by the time she lay down. She was tired too. She took a quick shower, threw on a shirt, and lay down next to Ray. She could hear his even breathing as he slept. Normally Brandy slept with her, but tonight she was banished to her bed on the floor. Stella tried to give Ray his space, but he reached over, pulled her closer, and fell back asleep. Stella could get used to this every night. It wasn't long before sleep found her, but not before she thought about the figure she had seen earlier.

Stella was tossing and turning in her sleep, and Ray felt her. She was talking and moving her head back and forth as if she were trapped.

"Baby, wake up, my love. It's just a dream." She didn't hear him. "My love, wake up. It's ok. I'm here." Just then Stella jolted awake with a scream. She was drenched in sweat. She looked at him, breathing hard. "It's ok, ma. I'm here. Don't worry." She nodded and lay back down in his arms. "I hate this. I hate that you had your sanity taken from you. That you were disrespected, beaten, and violated. I need you to feel safe with me." Ray looked so upset.

"Babe, there's nothing you can do," Stella said taking a deep breath. She turned to look at him. "I told Ma what happened when I got back from Cali."

"How did she take it?"

"She did her best to hold the dramatics. But I guess the way any mom would. I told her about the move, and she wished us the best of luck in our future and said to bring her grandbabies." Stella smiled at the idea. Ray tightened his hold on her. He needed her to feel safer. Her back was against his chest.

She needed to feel closer to him and pushed back and grinded against him. She heard him moan in her ear. His erection was always present and ready when she was near. He kissed her neck, and she reached behind her to pull his head tighter against her. He pulled her underwear down and entered her from behind. He had his hand on her hip as he slid in and out of her. He felt so good, and she never wanted him to stop. Everything he did, he did it slowly to make sure she was ok with any movements he made. She could feel her orgasm building, and she grabbed his arm. He knew when she was about to come. "That's it, ma. Cum for me, baby," he whispered in her ear. He could feel her tightening around him. She cried out, and he came with her in an explosive orgasm that he had been building up over the last few weeks. They both shivered and slowed down. They lay together, facing each other, for a few minutes before Stella got up to use the bathroom. She got back in bed, and put his hand against her heart. He placed himself in her arms with his head on her shoulder. She held him tight, feeling his breathing getting even again. They both fell asleep.

Chapter 33

The next day Stella got ready to see Kay. She texted Kay and let her know she would be there soon. Since they were both going to Brooklyn, Ray and Stella shared a cab. The cab dropped Stella off first, and she kissed Ray and let him know she would meet him later at his mom's.

When Stella walked into Kay's apartment, she couldn't remember ever seeing Kay have such a mess. "What the hell happened in here?" Kay just sat on the sofa looking defeated. Stella had had no idea just how hard Kay was taking this separation from Seb.

"Look…" Kay told Stella and pointed at the coffee table. Stella walked over and saw five pregnancy tests. All positive. She sat down slowly and looked at Kay. Kay had tears running down her face. "I thought we were being careful, but that one time we weren't, his super sperm did this. What am I going to do?"

Stella was in shock. "First of all, how is this possible so soon? We just got back. Second, Did you tell him?"

Kay shook her head no. "I knew we didn't use protection that last time and I was on high alert. I said let me see if it comes up and sure enough here we are. This isn't something I wanted to tell him over FaceTime. I have to go see him and tell him in person. I don't even know if I want to keep it. Am I ready for this? You know what's crazy—a part of me wants to be with him and start a family, but what if that's not what he wants? This is happening so fast. We won't even have time to enjoy each other."

Stella hugged Kay and held her tight. "It's gonna be ok. Listen—I'm here regardless of what decision you make. But Seb is a good guy, and the looks he was giving you back in San Diego were not just fling looks. And remember, this is not just some random guy. We've known him for seven years, and we all used to hang out all the time. I'm sure you will work this out and it'll be ok." Kay nodded her head. Stella got up and started fixing up the apartment. "Let's get you outta this apartment and grab a bite to eat. Go get dressed."

Kayla got up and went to her room. Stella busied herself around the house. She took the pregnancy tests and put them in a ziplock bag. She heard Kay's phone ringing, and then it went silent, but she didn't hear Kay talking. Stella's phone pinged. It was a text from Seb.

Seb: Hey Stel, have you heard from Kay? I'm trying to call her, and she's not answering

Kay was looking at her from the bedroom. "You know you're going to have to talk to him eventually, right?" Stella asked. Kay nodded. Stella typed out a reply.

Stella: Hey Seb, I'm with her now. She's getting dressed so we can have a girls' day. How's everything?

"I told him we're having a girls' day," Stella said, and Kay gave a thumbs-up and went to comb her hair. Stella's phone pinged again.

Seb: Everything is good. Just missing your girl. This love thing is crazy.

Stella's eyes opened wide. He loved Kayla too. He was going to be super excited about the coming baby! Stella felt all warm inside for them.

Stella: Yup that's what it feels like

She hit send and put the phone in her pocket so she could wash dishes.

The girls went out to brunch and came to an agreement that Kayla had to go to LA. They spoke about the inevitability of Stella moving out there and how they could all be together and help raise the baby. It did take a village, after all. Kay was on the fence about making such a big move. Maybe once she found out how Seb really felt about her being pregnant, she could make a real decision.

Kayla texted Seb and said she was going out there to visit him ASAP. His response was exactly what Kayla wanted. He couldn't wait. Would he still feel like that after she told him she was pregnant? Only time would tell. They agreed she should drink no alcohol since she was pregnant. It already sounded as if she intended to keep the baby, which made Stella happy. That kid was going to be beautiful and spoiled rotten.

They ordered their favorite foods—chicken wings and french fries. When the food came, Stella saw Kayla's face shift at the sight. Uh-oh. Kayla looked at the food and the smell was getting to her.

"My sense of smell is already reaching peak levels. What the hell! He impregnated me with a 3 month old fetus. He's going to pay for doing this to me," she said with a pout.

Stella chuckled. "Ok, let's find you something you can stomach."

Chapter 34

Later that evening, after Stella made sure Kayla got home ok, she headed to Ray's mom's house. Ray opened the door with a big smile on his face. His mom, Maria, ran over to her to give her a hug and a kiss. It had been a long time since they had seen each other. The house smelled like Puerto Rican heaven. Maria was cooking her ass off for her baby. Freestyle music was playing, and Ray started twirling Stella until she was dizzy and almost fell over. He steadied her, and they laughed. Maria had a big smile. She seemed so thrilled to see her son and Stella together again and so happy.

Maria was a short, slim beautiful woman. You could tell she got any guy she wanted now and when she was younger. She had that confidence about her. Stella guessed raising a boy into the kind of man Ray had grown up to be was reason enough to be confident. Maria had long hair that she dyed dark red. Her skin was an olive color, which was where Ray got his complexion.

"Mamita, come, come. *Vente*. Sit. How's everything?" Maria asked Stella as they sat on the sofa in the living room. Stella gave her the rundown of everything that was going on and how excited she was for Ray.

"Ay, *mija*, we are so proud and excited for him too." Maria looked like such a proud mom. Seeing her baby living the dream was something every mother wanted. Stella looked over at Ray and smiled. He hated when his mom doted on him, and he almost rolled his eyes but caught himself.

"Hey. No eye rolling!" Maria yelled at him, and he laughed. "I can still give you a *boffeta* (a smack) no matter how old you are. You're never too old." Ray knew she meant that. His mother didn't play when it came to respect. He had run from the *chancla* many times in his life.

"How's Kay?" he asked, and she wanted to tell him the truth, but it wouldn't be fair for him to know and not be able to tell Seb.

"She's good. She's making plans to go see Seb this week."

"Oh, that's awesome. At least she can keep him company while I'm here. I leave on Sunday."

"Yeah, yeah, just dampen the mood," she said playfully and with an eye roll. She was just thankful she had him for a week. She looked at the time. "I'm going to head home soon to take Brandy out for a walk. She must be going nuts."

Maria announced, "Food is ready," and boy was it. She had made all the Puerto Rican staples: rice and beans, mofongo, *pernil.* Ray and Stella ate until they couldn't anymore. There just wasn't anything like a home-cooked meal. It was better than any fancy dish at any fancy restaurant. Stella stayed for another hour and then said her goodbyes.

Maria took her in an embrace and whispered in her ear, "I'm so happy he's back with you. You are the only one he's meant to be with." And she gave Stella a kiss on the cheek. Stella nodded, at a loss for words. She hadn't realized how much she missed that woman. Maria was like having a second mom.

She turned to Ray and told him he should stay if he wanted, but all he wanted was to go home with her and Brandy. He loved that dog. She was so cute and loving, like her mom.

They said their goodbyes and left with plates of food. As predicted, Brandy was going crazy when they got home. Stella put her harness and leash on and handed the leash to Ray. They closed the door behind them and started to walk. Ray was holding Brandy's leash in one hand and Stella's hand in the other.

This was the life, he thought to himself. In a flash he had an image of them walking the dog with a baby carriage. Hopefully soon, he thought. The nagging thought of telling Stella what he needed to tell her was at the back of his mind, but he had all week. He just wanted to enjoy this.

Chapter 35

Their week was going by fast. Kayla had left to see Seb on Wednesday and was coming back on Sunday. Stella was on pins and needles about how their conversation would go.

Seb picked Kay up at the airport. They ran to each other as if they hadn't seen each other in years. God, she had missed him. Seb picked her up while he was hugging her, and she laughed. She felt like a teenager when she was with him. Free and in love.

"Hi, my queen," he said.

"Hi, baby," she replied, and they kissed. Seb grabbed her bag and headed for the short-term parking. They got the car and left the airport.

"Are you hungry, ma?" he asked. He really had no idea how hungry she was.

"Babe, I'm starving."

"Wanna order food or go out?"

"Let's just order. I'm exhausted." Not just from the flight, she thought. The drive was about thirty-five minutes. Kayla was taking in the sights, thinking she might live there one day.

He took her hand and kissed it. "I'm so happy you're here. I feel…whole again," he said, and he gave her a quick sideways look and smile. She loved him.

She prayed and prayed he would take this news ok. When those tests had all come back positive, she had panicked.

They arrived back at the apartment. It was nice here, she thought. Seb grabbed the menu for the Chinese food spot and passed it to Kay. When he was done ordering, he hung up the phone and walked over to her. She was nervous. How would she tell him? He sat with her on the sofa, and they started making out like teenagers. They were getting hot, but Kayla needed to tell him.

She pulled away from him, and he looked at her with heavy eyes.

"Seb," she started.

"Yeah, ma?" he said gruffly.

"I have to tell you something," she said, and his eyes opened wide. If she were breaking up with him, he would die, he thought.

"What's up, Kay?" He asked straightening up and looking nervous.

She grabbed his hands and kissed them. "Seb, I love you more than anything, and that's the reason why I had to fly out here so that I could speak to you in person." She stood up and walked over to her bag and pulled out the ziplock.

"I know we just got together, and if you want to run, I understand." He had a confused look on his face. She took a breath. "Seb, you're going to be a daddy," she said softly, handing him the ziplock bag. His face softened as the realization of what she had said sank in. He looked at the bag and looked at her. At the bag and at her. A big smile spread across his face. "Kay, are you serious?" he said quietly. She nodded, trying to gauge his reaction.

"This is the greatest news ever!!" he said, almost screaming, and she started crying and laughing at the same time. "I'm gonna be a DADDY!" he yelled, and Kay laughed. He grabbed her and kissed her hard. They took a picture together, him kissing her stomach. "Kay, this is amazing. I feel so blessed, and I'm so happy you came here to tell me in person so that we can CELEBRATE!" He picked her up and went running around the house. Kayla was cracking up. In that moment, she knew she had made the right decision to come tell him in person.

Chapter 36

At 8:30 p.m. a group message came in. It was the picture of Seb kissing Kayla's stomach. Stella put her hand over her mouth. Her eyes were watery at the sight of them looking so happy. Then she heard Ray yell, "WHAT!!!!" And he jumped up.

"Yup! You're gonna be an uncle!!"

"You knew!! And didn't tell me?" he said, pouting.

"I couldn't tell you before he knew!! I'm sorry!!!"

Stella sent four heart emojis and typed out

Stella: Congratulations, my brother and sister. I love you both so much and can't wait to meet my little niece or nephew.

Ray called Seb. She heard him say "Dude, congratulations. This is awesome," and he laughed on the phone.

Kay texted Stella separately.

Kay: Looks like I'm moving out here too!

Stella stopped and read and reread what Kay had said. And then she started jumping up and down, and Brandy started jumping up and down too, and Stella started laughing.

Ray hung up with Seb. "So she's moving to LA too. Great, at least we'll all have each other," he said, walking over and giving Stella a hug. "Do you ever think about kids?" he asked her. His face was serious and thoughtful.

"Yeah, sometimes recently," she said, looking up at him. "Do you?"

"All the time since the woman of my dreams finally came back into my life. Soooo how many should we have?" he asked, and she giggled.

"Let's get me to LA first, and then we can talk about baby number one."

Sunday came and Ray left. Stella started planning for the move.

When he got home, Seb asked him, "Did you tell her yet?" Ray shook his head no.

"It's going to be worse if she finds out another way," Seb said with a you-know-I'm-right look on his face. He was right. But everything was going so well. Ray just did not want to rock the boat.

Chapter 37
Two months later

I t was Stella's last day at work, and she said goodbye to all her coworkers, whom she was really fond of. The car was packed up. She and Kay decided they needed a hooptie to get them down there. They pooled their money and got a mini SUV so they could leave to LA together. Kayla's baby bump was small, but it was starting to show. Stella went with her to every appointment and updated Seb with FaceTime so he could feel like he was there. He swore from the sonogram that the baby looked like him already.

Stella changed in the bathroom into her jeans, sneakers, a Batman jersey, and a Batman hat. She went down and got the car. She thought she saw that figure across the street but looked again and it was gone. She shrugged. Her mind must have been playing tricks on her.

She picked up Kayla and Brandy, and they were on their way. They had various stops planned out on the way so they could all use the bathroom and sleep. They estimated it should take about seven or eight days. The guys were worried about them doing this long trip alone, but Stella insisted that they had it covered. The girls were smart about their stops, making sure they were always in public. Stella didn't want Kay to drive, so they made sure Stella had plenty of rest. Ray would text Kayla to make sure Stella was ok. Stella was determined to do this drive as quickly and as safely as possible. If she felt tired, they stopped. One of Stella's dreams was to go to Chicago and see the statue of Michael Jordan so they made sure that was one of their stops. Another stop they made was in Las Vegas at the Grand Canyon. It was a place they always wanted to see and their pictures were amazing. It was something to see in one's lifetime. Nature's beauty at its finest.

Stella had quickly secured a job at a law firm, thanks to a call from her boss, and was starting in a week. It was a sweet job starting at $65,000 a year, which was what Stella had been making before, so there was no gap in salary. Ray and Seb got a second apartment outside LA since Seb would be living with Kay and Stella with Ray and Brandy. It was a coordinated effort on everyone's part to get this move done as smoothly as possible. They arrived at the new apartment right outside LA and parked. The guys were standing out front to meet them. Stella was dead tired, and Kay was starving, which they all knew, so the guys had food waiting for them. For tonight they were all staying together. Ray and Stella would stay at the apartment in LA since it was closer to the studio for him and the law firm for her. Seb and Kay would stay in this new apartment, which was only twenty minutes away from his job, so it worked out for everybody.

Stella looked at Seb and Kay with admiration. The love they had in their eyes for each other and the way he touched her stomach made Stella's heart ache. She couldn't wait to have that with Ray.

Brandy lost it when she saw Ray. He picked her up, and she kissed him all over.

Everything revolved around the baby for everybody now. Seb had added Kay to his medical insurance plan at his job, so Kay was already set up to see a doctor in Arcadia. They took Kayla's belongings inside and were about to eat when Ray's phone pinged. He looked down at his phone, frowned, replied, and put his phone back in his pocket quickly.

"Everything ok?" Stella asked him.

He didn't want to make eye contact with her. "Yeah, ma, everything is good."

She had just driven for eight and a half days. If Ray was already hiding something, she would feel like an idiot. Stella gave Kay a look. Kay looked at her as if to say she had noticed too but shrugged and kept moving about. Stella was starting to feel uneasy. He was hiding something, and she could feel it. After all that driving, she couldn't think straight and just needed to sleep. She didn't want to fly off the handle for no reason. Stella always tried her best to keep her temper under control and let cooler heads prevail. Hear all the facts before losing her shit.

Seb and Ray had purchased beds for them to sleep on. Stella crashed so hard that night with Ray lying next to her, watching her sleep and hoping she hadn't caught on about his text earlier. The engagement ring that he had ordered for her was delayed, and it pissed him off. He just wanted to propose to her already and make sure she knew how much he loved her. He had gotten his check for the Disney movie, and it was more than anything he had ever done before. Filming had wrapped last week, and Vincent was sending him out on auditions again to get the next big thing lined up for him. He would be comfortable for a while without anything lined up, but he knew the first thing he wanted to do was get Stella a ring that she deserved. It was a beautiful princess cut diamond. He couldn't wait to propose to her. His decisions while trying to get over Stella at the forefront of his mind. Everytime he wanted to tell her, he lost his his nerve.

Seb was ready to propose to Kayla too. That baby had changed everything. Ray couldn't wait to have babies with Stella. He just wanted to make sure they were married first and had a solid foundation for their children. But the way they would be humping like bunnies, marriage would probably come afterward.

Chapter 38

Stella started working at the new law firm and proved herself to be everything her boss had said she was. The hours were 8:00 a.m. to 4:00 p.m., which was better than nine to five. Ray was back at the Disney studios doing some voice corrections for his movie, which now had a name: *Penny's Mission*. She was so excited for him. This was a big, big deal. The plan was for the movie to be released sometime in 2024. From what she understood, there was tons of postproduction that had to be done.

On the Friday after Stella started working, she headed to the studio to pick Ray up. She parked, and as she walked in, she noticed Ray talking to a blond woman who was laughing a bit too loudly and flirtatiously for her liking. She told herself to relax because this was Ray's place of work. She had to close her eyes and *woosaaa*.

He saw her and immediately started walking toward her. Blondie walked away. He gave her a kiss. "Hey, ma," he said with a smile, and she relaxed. If he was going to be a star, she would have to put her big-girl pants on and learn how to deal with the attention he was going to get, which she hated. She was Puerto Rican and was jealous. She couldn't help it.

"How was work?" he asked her as they walked out toward the car.

"It was good. All the coworkers are nice. No one has said a thing about my accent," she was proud to say. Everywhere she went, somebody always asked her where she was from. It was what it was. "I'm hoping I can move up from assistant to something else. I don't want to be stagnant in a position."

"Yeah, I get it," He said.

Since Stella and Kay had gotten there, they had fallen into a rhythm and routine with the guys. Kay needed to make some money, but she didn't want to get a full-time job while pregnant and then have to take leave. Not to mention, who would hire her at three months pregnant? Kay understood it was against the law to discriminate against pregnant women but she also understood, there was a unspoken unethical rule about not hiring pregnant people and people over 50.

Five weeks after they got there, Kay decided to start delivering with Amazon Flex and DoorDash. Seb was worried about her being out delivering, but nobody was going to stop her. Kay had always worked, and being in this new place was jarring, even with her support system. She was applying for work-from-home jobs as an accountant, since she had her degree, and she was hoping something would click. Stella was already buying the baby some clothes, and Kay needed to start getting the baby furniture.

Seb had applied for an upper-management position within Mattel so he could get a bump in pay too. He was so excited for the baby. His dad hadn't been around, so he wanted to make sure he was part of everything. In two weeks, they would find out the baby's sex. He wanted a boy. Kay wanted a girl.

He would find out soon whether he was being considered for the new position. Either way he needed to make more money. He had never in a million years thought he would be having a baby, and especially not with Kay, whom he had been pining for back when Ray and Stella were together the first time, though he was already in a relationship that had lasted too long. He had to make sure she never regretted making such a big move. If Stella weren't out here, he wasn't sure whether she would have made a huge move like this. He was so thankful she hadn't balked when he brought up her moving out to Cali. It would have been difficult to raise a baby from three thousand miles away.

Chapter 39

Kay called Stella to come help her do her rounds that Saturday. There were some areas that Kay wasn't familiar with yet, and she wanted company. Well, it was that and the fact that Ray needed time to plan everything for tonight. The girls were out for about six hours delivering for Amazon Flex.

"How do you feel?" Stella asked Kay.

"I feel great. Tired all the time. And hungry! Let me not forget hungry."

They had stopped to grab a bite on the way. Everything had been delivered, so they could head back. Stella was driving, and Kay was messing with the music on her phone. They had about forty-five minutes to get back home. That Amazon Flex work felt exhausting—just driving all day, Stella thought. Maybe it was just exhaustion from the day, but her stomach was killing her. Probably from the food they had eaten.

"Kay, my stomach is killing me. Not like a regular stomachache. Like a legit pain. Do you feel ok?"

"I feel fine. Do you want to pull over?" Kay looked at her with a frown.

"I'm going to try to make it to a rest stop." Stella was driving on a mission but didn't want to make Kay feel unsafe. The pain was getting worse. Stella squinted and let out a growl. Kayla looked at her, concerned. "Kay, I think I need to go to the hospital," Stella told her as soon as she made it to the rest stop.

Kay changed the GPS to go to the nearest hospital, and they switched so Kay could drive. Stella had never felt anything like this before. What the hell was happening? The hospital was ten minutes away. She called Ray to tell him and he told her they were on their way. They arrived at the hospital and checked in. Stella's underwear felt wet, and she knew something was going on. As she waited for the nurse to call her to the back, she went to the bathroom. Sure enough, she was bleeding. She cleaned herself up and put on a pantyliner she found in her purse. She couldn't think straight through the pain to remember when her last period was.

"Kay, I'm bleeding," she whispered to Kay when she got back.

Kayla was worried. "Your period?" she asked.

Stella shrugged. "I'm not sure." With the moving and everything, Stella hadn't even noticed that her period was late. Maybe that's all this was. But those pains weren't cramps. They called Stella to the back, and Kay went with her until Ray got there. They had her put on a gown, examined her, took blood, and said they would be back.

Ray and Seb got there after what felt like an eternity for Ray. Stella told Seb to take Kay home so she could rest and said they would be in touch. Seb and

Kay were hesitant to leave. "Don't worry. I'm ok. Go," Stella reassured them.

Seeing Stella in that hospital bed made Ray nauseous. When Seb and Kay left, Ray turned to Stella with concerned eyes. He grabbed her hand, kissed it, and held it tight. Stella's emotions were off the chart. She thought she knew what they were going to say, but she wanted to hear it from them. She told him what she was feeling and then noticed Ray was all dressed up. "Were you guys going to go out?"

"You and I were going to go out," he said, and Stella felt bad.

"I'm so sorry. Ughh, this sucks. You look so hot," she said, touching his face.

"Least of my worries right now," he said, his face was full of worry. "I don't like seeing you like this in the hospital."

Just then the doctor came in—a female doctor whose badge said "Dr. Sawyer." "Hi, Stella. I'm Dr. Sawyer," she started, pulling up a chair to sit next to Stella. "So your blood work and everything came back." She was talking in a low, soothing voice, and Stella already knew what had happened. "There's no easy way to say this." Dr. Sawyer took a breath and said, "You're in the middle of having a miscarriage." Stella felt Ray's hand squeeze hers, and her tears just started falling. Dr. Sawyer grabbed Stella's other hand, knowing she had just delivered devastating news. Hearing the words was so much worse than having them in your head.

Dr. Sawyer continued. "I am so sorry," she said, and she had genuine pain behind her eyes. "At this point, your body just has to go through the motions on its own for the next few hours. We are going to send you home. I will give you some pads to put on. The pain meds should also last for a few hours, but I will prescribe you more just in case. Here's my card. You can follow up with me or your primary doctor in a couple of weeks to make sure there's nothing residual remaining and to check and see whether there are any steps you must take to avoid miscarrying in the future. I would say that you have an elevated risk from here on out, so just always take precautions if you are trying to get pregnant again."

She let go of Stella's hand and got up to leave. She turned around and said, "I've been through it too. I know what you must be feeling." She paused for a beat and walked out.

Stella finally looked at Ray, and the tears in his eyes finished destroying her. She cried as if she were five years old. She had to compose herself. She just wanted to go home and crawl into bed. Dr. Sawyer came back with the discharge papers, pads, and the script for the pain meds. Stella got dressed, and they walked out slowly, Ray holding her tightly to him. They got into the car and started the long drive home.

Ray spoke for the first time. "I don't even know what I'm feeling right now. This pain is unlike anything I've ever felt."

"I should have known, and I didn't. Between the moving and the new job and getting situated here, I didn't even realize my period never came. I checked my calendar, and I should have gotten it two weeks ago. It's my fault for not being on top of it." Stella hated herself right now.

"Nope. Don't do that. It's not your fault. Ma, it just means that it's not our time yet, that's all. Nobody's fault." And she knew he was right, but she wouldn't let it go. He squeezed her hand and brought it to his lips, even though he was distraught, and she hated herself for bringing this pain on him.

She let Kay and Seb know what was going on through the group chat. She just stared out the window. What if she couldn't carry? What if Ray eventually really wanted a baby and she couldn't carry? She had just moved her whole life across the country together with her best friend, and she was broken. She hated herself and could feel herself falling into a deep depression. It was as if she had been destined for pain. Her dad, Ray leaving, Jason, the baby. She just didn't know how much more she could take. Her mother always said, "God wouldn't give you more than you can handle." Well, God was certainly pushing his or her luck. They got home, and she went straight to the shower.

She stood under the shower just bleeding. She heard Ray enter the bathroom.

He undressed and got into the shower with her. He wrapped his arms around her, and she lost it. She cried and Ray cried silently with her. They got out of the shower, and Ray dried her off. She had to put on that ridiculous heavy absorbent pad to catch the rest of her baby, she thought. He helped her get into bed, and she closed her eyes. She felt Ray lie next to her. He held her tightly as she fell asleep. She was exhausted and couldn't deal with life right now.

"I'm right here, ma," she heard him say, and she felt him kiss her forehead.

Ray was destroyed. All he knew was that he had to be strong for Stella. She was in bad shape. Dr. Sawyer had let them know that Stella would need time to recuperate from this. Physically, emotionally, and mentally. He knew Stella was going to fight him about going to work on Monday. Depending on what happened tonight, he would decide how to approach it with her. He had never expected this day to turn out this way. He had anticipated being engaged by the end of the night. He had never thought in a million years that he would be losing a child. He texted Stella's mom to let her know what was going on, and she had the obvious reaction. She said she was flying out on the next flight, but Ray assured her Stella was well cared for. Kay had offered to come over earlier, while they were driving home, but Stella had shot her down.

Stella was always thinking about everyone else and never put herself first. This time she had to put herself first, and she was still trying to shield everyone's feelings. The loss of this baby was something neither one of them would get over.

Chapter 40

At about 11:00 p.m., Stella started shifting and making noises. She got up, visibly in pain, and starting crying. The pain meds had worn off. "Ray," she moaned. "Pain meds, please!" she begged him. Ray had picked up the pills while she was asleep just in case. It was a good thing he was always steps ahead. He gave her the two pills per the instructions, and she took them. It was a long ten minutes before the meds fully kicked in. She could feel herself bleeding, and she lay in Ray's arms silently crying.

"Ray, I'm so sorry," she sobbed into his shoulder, and the only thing he could do was hold her.

"My love…you don't have to apologize. You did nothing wrong," Ray tried reassuring her, but he knew his words were falling on deaf ears. When they say "for better or worse," this must be considered the *worse* part, he thought. Ray would have done anything to take away everything she was going through. Stella nodded and fell back asleep. She felt so heavy. This must be the exhaustion the doctor had told her she would feel.

She woke up again sometime in the middle of the night and needed Ray. She reached out for him and whispered, "Babe…I have to use the bathroom to change this thing." She felt so helpless and hated it. Everything felt heavy. Even her body when she tried to move. At least she didn't have pain. Ray grabbed her with strong hands and helped her into the bathroom. After she removed her underwear, she just stared, and Ray was by her side.

Stella looked at Ray. "Does this end, pa?," she said, looking so defeated.

"It will, my love. I promise. If we have each other…everything will be fine."

Stella believed him and nodded. She cleaned herself off, put another pad on, and went back out to the bedroom. They fell back asleep quickly.

Chapter 41

They woke up at around 8:00 a.m. that morning. Stella was thankful she had had a peaceful sleep. There had been no signs of anyone's face. That was the last thing she needed on top of everything else. Ray had let Seb know that he needed a mental break and asked whether they could come over. There was a knock on the door at 2:00 p.m. Ray went to open it. Kay and Seb walked in, and Kay went straight to throw herself next to Stella. Seb came and gave Stella a long hug. He had turned into the brother she had always wanted. "I wanted to come last night. How are you feeling?" Kay asked.

Stella shook her head. "Nah, it's ok. We were in a bad place last night."

Ray came and sat next to her. He gave her a kiss on the cheek. "Are you ok if I step out for a bit with Seb?"

"Yeah, babe, it's ok." She knew he needed to decompress after everything. "Just be careful." He kissed her and lingered. The two men left, and Stella stood with Kay. She felt exhausted and just wanted to lie down. Kay cooked a hot meal and ate for both of them since Stella couldn't keep anything down. At least Ray would have something to eat when he got back.

Kayla sat next to Stella and asked "Do you want to talk about it?" Stella just shook her head no. She felt the tears coming up again and just held them at bay. Kayla wrapped her arm around Stella and they watched TV mindlessly. Kay knew when she just needed to be there physically but not verbally. She knew Stella better than anyone.

Ray and Seb just drove around aimlessly. Guys had an unusual way of expressing themselves. Seb had no idea what to say, so he just drove to a bar. They walked in and sat down. The bartender came over and took their order. Seb had a soda, but he ordered a Jack and Coke for Ray, knowing he needed something stronger. "So much for being engaged right now, huh?" Ray said. Seb shook his head.

"Remember how our parents always said everything happens for a reason? I guess that's the best way to think about it." Seb wanted to be sensitive, especially since Kay was pregnant and everything was going smoothly for them.

Ray nodded. "Yes, that's what I told Stel last night. She's beating herself up for not knowing, and all I can do is watch. It's driving me crazy. Seb, I can't even explain the feeling of that doctor telling us news like that. I don't wish this on my worst enemy."

"Dude, I can't even imagine." Seb couldn't imagine. If something happened to his baby, he would lose it.

By the time they left, Ray was drunk, and Seb had to get him home. They got back to the apartment, and Ray stumbled into the bedroom where Kay and Stel were sitting and watching TV. Kay and Seb said their goodbyes. Once they left, Ray lay down and put his head on Stella's shoulder. Stella understood why he had been drinking. At this point, she'd have killed for a drink. He was drowning his sorrows. Stella kissed his forehead and could feel the waterworks coming again, but she fought them. And lost. Ray turned his head toward her and kissed her. He tasted like pure Jack and Coke. He just needed to take her pain away. He threw all his drunken love behind the kiss. It was an intimate moment for both of them and something Stella hadn't even known she needed. The closeness to him, feeling him. He broke away, breathing hard. "We'll be ok, Stel," he said quietly, and she nodded in agreement. How could she go to work tomorrow? She still didn't feel 100 percent, but she had to pull her weight. Ray assured her she didn't have to, but she just couldn't come to terms with having somebody taking care of her. She always did it herself. She had nothing holding her back now, she thought…might as well just work and get that paper. But she had to be careful because she was tired and still bleeding slightly.

Chapter 42

"Are you sure you want to go?" Ray was concerned the following morning. Stella kept pushing herself, and he knew it was because of the move and trying to get used to a new city, in a new relationship and a new job.

She nodded. "Yeah, I got this. I took a vitamin C pill to give me a boost, and barring anything crazy happening, I'll be ok. If I stay here, I will go crazy. Better to stay busy." She knew he was worried. But she reassured him. The only thing that worried her was getting her health insurance to kick in so she could have that follow-up. Stella knew she should stay home, but she didn't want to wallow. She had to be strong for both herself and Ray.

Stella got through the day without any hiccups. She felt better than she had the past couple of days. Sandra, Ray, Seb, and Kay were all texting her non-stop. She was so grateful for the support system she had. She knew most people were not so fortunate. The next item on her agenda was to make up for this weekend she had ruined for Ray. She had an epiphany at work and decided she wanted to do something nice for him once she was free and clear in the next week or so.

Stella got home and started cooking. Ray was out running errands. There was a knock at the door, and she thought Ray had forgotten his key, though he had never mentioned anything. She checked the peephole and saw a girl standing there. Stella opened the door apprehensively.

The girl was about Stella's height, with thick hips, big boobs, brown hair, and brown eyes.

"Hi, can I help you?" Stella asked.

"Hi. Is Ray here?" the girl asked. Stella's hairs stood up.

"No, he's not. May I ask who you are?" Stella said, trying not to give this girl an attitude because she didn't want to jump to conclusions.

"I'm his ex-wife, Amanda. I have some of his mail that came to my house, and I just wanted to drop it off since I was in the area."

Stella froze, and Amanda noticed. Stella took the mail from her, and Amanda walked away. Had this chick smirked as she walked away? What had just happened? Ex-wife? This motherfucker was married?? Stella thought.

What a week this was turning out to be. So much for doing something nice for his ass.

"*PUÑETA COÑO!*" Stella screamed. Ray was in trouble once Stella started cursing in Spanish.

Chapter 43

Ray had lined up another job, and Vincent was riding high with him. This was the fastest any talent he had was getting jobs. And good-paying ones, which Ray was happy about. He would start filming in a month, so he wanted to spend as much time with Stella as he could. The filming days were long, twelve-to-fourteen-hour days. He knew she would be asleep by the time he came home. He was hoping to make enough that she wouldn't have to work, but getting her to stop would be a whole other problem. Little did he know the problem he had waiting for him at home.

Ray walked in, and Stella was sitting on the sofa with the mail on her lap, "Honey, I'm hoommme," he said with a smile, trying to lighten the mood after what they had just gone through. Stella was not having it. Ray's face turned down. "What's going on?"

"Who's Amanda?" And she waited for him to answer incorrectly so she could go crazy. She had just moved across the country for some dick she hadn't had in four years. She kept calling herself an idiot. Ray walked slowly toward her.

He saw her face and hung his head. "She's my ex-wife. We were married for about six months when

I was feeling low about everything here two years ago." At least he didn't lie, she thought.

"*Maldita sea* Ray! How could you not tell me? I'm not a moron. I know you had a life for four years. We were not together. You were entitled to be with whomever you wanted." It made Stella nauseated just thinking about it. Her stomach was starting to hurt, and she winced. She needed to get out of there. She got up and grabbed her jacket.

"You know what sucks, Ray? A chunk of my trust in you has just withered away. I told you what happened to me the first moment we were alone because it was important for you to know. You didn't think having a wife was something I should know? It was the icing on the cake I needed after the past few days, not to mention the past four years," she said, and she walked out slamming the door.

Ray heard Stella yell "*CARAJO!*" in the hallway. Brandy looked up at Ray with judging eyes. He couldn't talk. Stella was right. He should have told her. There was no excuse. He would give her the space he knew she needed to cool off. This week of all weeks she had to find out. Ray had wanted to tell her but was afraid she wouldn't come to LA if she knew. Stella had always been the first woman he wanted to propose to, and the fact that she was now going to be the second had to hurt. Even though they hadn't been together for four years, that didn't mean the thought of each other with other people didn't make them uneasy.

Stella went to the dog park where she went with Brandy and just sat by herself, tears falling. How could Ray have kept this from her? She felt as if her heart were a thousand pounds. She was supposed to be his wife first, and she hated herself for feeling this way. She had known he wouldn't wait for her forever. They were never supposed to get back together. It was divine fate that had brought them back together. Her stomach was hurting, but she was not going to any hospital. She would deal with it. The bitch had showed up with mail and a smirk. The gall, Stella thought. Ugh. She didn't even look like Ray's type. Her face looked so familiar. It didn't matter.

Just then a puppy without a leash ran up to her, and Stella picked her up. The puppy couldn't have been more than six or eight months and was super playful. Stella read her name tag. "Bella," it said, and there was a phone number. Stella heard someone yelling "Bella" from across the park. She walked with the dog in her arms toward the yelling. Just then Stella saw a tall figure coming toward her. As he got closer, Stella was able to make out his features. He had short brown hair and blue eyes. He was wearing gray sweats and a black pullover hoodie. Stella waved at him, and he came toward them. She thought to herself that she should be much more careful.

"Oh my God, you got her!! Thank you so much."

His face was clear now, and Stella could see how handsome he was. She passed Bella to her owner, who put her too-big harness on her and was attempting to adjust the size. "It's no problem. She came right up to me, and I grabbed her." Stella laughed. The guy looked down at Stella.

"How can I ever repay you?" He was tall. Stella estimated he was six foot three. He had a big, muscular body. His brown hair and blue eyes contrasted against his white skin. He had a goatee and beard.

"It's no problem. She's a beauty. I can see why you named her Bella," Stella said, petting the dog.

"My name is Shawn, by the way," he said, sticking his hand out.

"Stella," she said, and she shook his hand. Nothing there. It didn't matter who it was. She knew where and to whom her heart belonged.

"Sounds like Bella," he said with a smile, and Stella laughed.

"I got to get going. I'm glad I could return her to you. Adjust her harness so she doesn't slip out again."

"Yes, I think that's where I'm failing this dog," he said with a laugh, still struggling to adjust the harness.

"May I?" Stella asked, taking the puppy from him, and she went about making Bella's harness tighter. "That should do it." Bella licked her face, and Stella gave her a kiss.

"Thanks so much again! I thought I lost her forever."

"No problem," Stella said, and she turned around to walk away.

Ray was standing there with Brandy, watching.

He hesitantly walked up to Stella, and she met him halfway. His face held all the pain she felt.

"Stel, I'm so sorry. I should have told you. I didn't know how."

"Ray, you had a life before we found each other again. I must accept what it is. Seeing that girl on my stoop saying she was your ex-wife was terrible. I don't think I can handle anything else this week," she said, and she winced again.

Ray saw her face. "What's going on, Stel?"

"It's nothing. I'm exhausted," Stella said, and Ray looked at her.

"Are you sure?" he asked.

"Yeah, it's just the stress from everything today and the last few days. I just want to lie down." Stella paused and continued speaking. "I'm going to stay with Kay and Seb tonight. I need some time to digest everything that's been happening. Kay is coming to pick me up. I just never thought you would keep something like this from me. Imagine if the roles were reversed. How would you feel?"

Ray put his head down. When he lifted his head, his nostrils were flaring. "I would be angry too," he said in a low voice.

"Yeah I know you would be. That's why I need some time to myself, to make sure I made the right decision moving out here. After what happened with Jason, I had no trust left in anybody but you and Kay."

He closed his eyes and shook his head. "I'm sorry," he said as Kayla pulled up. A tear rolled down Stella's face as she turned and walked toward the car. Ray couldn't move and Stella looked at him as they drove away.

Stella lay on the sofa that night contemplating if she had made the right decision moving to LA. She was so sure that Ray was what she wanted. Did she blind herself into thinking that just because of their history? The pain she felt in her heart of not having him or Brandy near her right now at this moment assured her that home was where she wanted to be. It was just the thought of Ray being intimate and saying he loved someone else that was hurting her more right now. Based on the smirk on Amanda's face before she left, Stella's expression of shock was the exact reaction Amanda was looking for. What a bitch. What if Amanda still wanted Ray? Worse yet, what if Ray decides later on that he wants her back? The thought was making Stella hyperventilate. Taking deep breaths, Stella got up to get a glass of water. She heard her phone ping as she sat back down. She looked at the text from Ray.

Ray: We miss you ma.

Stella looked at the text. She missed them too. She blew out a breath. She was twenty-seven years old and needed to get a grip on reality. As she stated, they were separated for four years. It was her decision mainly to let him go to LA alone and pursue his dream. She couldn't hold this against him. No matter how much it hurt. It wasn't his fault she never moved on after he left. She could have easily had a past as well but she chose not to. Because she only wanted him. He wasn't perfect. Nobody was perfect but Ray was pretty close and she knew he didn't mean to hurt her on purpose. It probably would've been less devastating if she hadn't just lost his child.

With that thought, she decided to respond.

Stella: I miss you too. I'll be home in the morning to get ready for work.

In her haste to get out of the apartment and away from Ray, Stella forgot to bring clothes for the following day. Not wanting to wake Kay and Seb, Stella slipped out in the morning making sure to close the door using her set of keys. It was 6:30am when Stella climbed out of the uber and walked into her apartment. Brandy started barking which startled Ray awake who was asleep on the sofa. Stella looked at them both. This was her little family and nobody was going to separate them. Ray slowly stood up and walked toward her.

"We didn't handle you not being here well at all last night," he said coming to stand in front of her.

He looked tired. Stella was exhausted. She came to depend on his body being next to hers every night so she didn't sleep either.

"I didn't handle it so well either. I'm sleepy. Hopefully the day goes by fast so I can come home and lay down," she said looking up at him. She could tell he was hesitating to lean down and kiss her so she wrapped her arms around his waist and hugged him to let him know it was going to be ok. She heard him audibly sigh and he held her tight. She pulled away and he leaned down to kiss her.

"I love you Stel."

"I love you more Ray. But if you ever hold anything back from me again, *te lo juro que te voy a mandar pal mismo carajo*." And with the serious facial expression she had on, Ray held up his hands. Her Spanish flowed when she meant what she had to say. He knew she meant it when she said that she would send him straight to hell if he ever held anything back from her again.

Stella broke away from him and started getting ready for her day.

Chapter 44

The day dragged and Stella was exhausted. Stella took a shower when she got home. She was bleeding a little more than she had been, but nothing crazy. It was probably just residual blood and tissue that had to come out. The initial pain had gone away, which was good. She and Ray sat together on the sofa watching TV. Her head on his shoulder. Ray holding her close. Brandy sitting close by Stella's side.

There was one nagging question on Stella's mind. She had to ask it and move on. "Ray…did you love Amanda?"

Ray turned and looked at her. "I thought I did. After a couple of months, I realized what a mistake I had made and was honest with her. She was pissed at first. After a while she seemed to understand that my heart was elsewhere. Especially since I kept calling her Stella. I could never love anybody the way that I love you. It was always supposed to be you. And you were right that we weren't together for four years, but it just didn't feel right. Nothing ever felt right. I wanted the pain of not having you go away, and it never did until I saw you."

Stella believed him. She had wanted to move on when he left but couldn't. He kissed Stella. They couldn't be intimate for obvious reasons. They kissed again, and this time the kiss lasted for what felt like hours. Neither one of them wanted it to end. They wanted to be connected as much as possible. "You're going to be my real and only wife, Stella," Ray told her passionately. She believed him when he said that too. Nobody had ever looked at her the way Ray did.

She had just moved 2,800 miles and upended her life for him. She had to give him the benefit of the doubt. "Ray, I don't want her to show up here ever again. Whatever mail you have can stay wherever it is. Is there anything else I need to know?"

Ray shook his head. "No. I promise."

Ray was counting his lucky stars Amanda hadn't ruined everything with Stella. He was beating himself up. He knew he needed to cut ties with Amanda; he just didn't want any drama. He called her and told her to just throw all the mail away. He also put in a request to have it forwarded just in case.

Chapter 45

Ray was starting his new movie in two weeks, and he wanted to be engaged before that. Stella had an appointment with Dr. Sawyer for the two-week follow-up, and he was anxious. He wanted to make sure she was ok before he started planning the engagement again. They arrived at the appointment, and they were both nervous. The nurse called them in, Stella put her gown on, and they waited for the doctor to come in.

Dr. Sawyer came in and started the examination. "How are you feeling, Stella?" Stella was holding Ray's hand.

"I'm ok. The bleeding finally stopped, and the pain went away." Dr. Sawyer nodded and continued the examination.

"So it looks as if you do not have any residual bleeding, which is good. No scarring or anything concerning."

Stella looked at Ray, who looked so relieved. "Ok, so what do we have to do now?" Stella asked.

"Well, if you want babies, I don't see any indication of problems moving forward. But you must be diligent and take care of yourself Stella. We want to make your next pregnancy go as smoothly as possible. I'm certain we'll get there," Dr. Sawyer said with a smile. Stella felt as if a weight had been lifted off her shoulders.

Dr. Sawyer made her feel at ease, and Stella knew she didn't want any other ob-gyn.

"Doc, quick question out of curiosity." Stella cleared her throat. "How fast can we start trying again?" Ray laughed, and Dr. Sawyer smiled.

"As soon as you leave here if you want," she said laughing. Stella laughed and gave a thumbs-up.

They walked out of the doctor's office relieved and happy. Stella had to go to work, but she really did not want to. Ray turned and gave her a big hug and kiss. "Well, that was great news. I was worried," he said.

"So was I," she said, blowing out a breath. "Ughhh, I don't want to go to work," she whined sticking out her bottom lip and pouting like a child. But she knew she had to go. Ray dropped her off and proceeded home. Tonight was the night he was going to propose. No more holding off. He had to go get things ready.

Chapter 46

Four o'clock couldn't come fast enough. Stella was dying to get home. There was only so much foreplay she could manage. She needed Ray in the worst way.

She got home, and the apartment was pitch black. She smelled chicken wings and french fries. There were candles everywhere. The dinner table held two candles and there were bottles of tequila and wine. Stella looked around while hanging her purse up on the hook near the door.

Ray was standing in front of the table wearing a full black three-piece suit, and he was holding a single peach rose. There were rose petals everywhere. She couldn't speak. "Die for You" by the Weeknd was playing in the background. He walked up to her slowly. He handed her the rose, and as she took it, he dropped down on one knee. He took the ring box out of his pocket and opened it. Stella couldn't move. Ray started speaking.

"Stella. My heart. My soul. My sun and my moon. I've dreamed of the moment I could finally do this. What I've learned over the past four years is that my life is incomplete without you. I want you to make me whole. I've loved you since the moment you stood next to me in Coney Island, and I want to be with you until the day I die. Please marry me."

Stella's tears were flowing. She was finally able to move, and she dropped to her knees in front of him and said, "Yes." With a big smile, he put the ring on her left hand. They hugged and kissed. "I love you, Ray," she said. They never wanted to let each other go. Brandy was jumping up and kissing them too. They laughed. He stood up and pulled her with him. They started slow dancing to the song. "This is all so beautiful. How did you have time?" Stella said in amazement at everything. It was so perfect. It was so them.

"Well, after I dropped you off, Seb and Kay came to help set everything up. I can't take all the credit," he said with a smile. "We should probably let them know, right?"

Stella grabbed her phone and took selfies of them in the usual way. One of them smiling and her holding her hand up, and one of Ray kissing her cheek while she held her hand up. They were beautiful pictures. She hit send to Seb and Kay and threw the phone to the side. She wanted Ray to herself. Now. She pulled him toward her, and they practically devoured each other.

"Wait, wait," Ray said, pulling away. "Shots or wine??"

"Shots! We have things to do." They laughed. Ray poured them shots and said, "To Mr. and Mrs. Garcia."

And Stella repeated, "To Mr. and Mrs. Garcia," and they knocked the shots back. While he was putting the glasses in the sink, she drank in the sight of him. That suit he had on was giving her life, she thought. She smiled. "What are you smiling at?" he asked, coming back toward her.

"Dirty, dirty, dirty thoughts, Ray!! That's what I'm smiling at!" They laughed and headed to the bedroom hand in hand.

Thank God it was Friday because Stella wanted to have her way with Ray all night long. They would be celebrating all weekend. The bedroom had more candles, and the music was following them somehow. The bed was covered in rose petals. She walked behind Ray and started removing his jacket. She placed it on the doorknob. Ray was unbuttoning his shirt slowly. She came and helped unbutton his shirt and pushed it over his shoulders. Lord, she was having a tough time containing herself. She didn't want to throw his shirt, but she threw his shirt. Looking at him standing there in his black tank top, black slacks, and black shoes was just killing her. He took her hand and led her into the bathroom. There were candles in there too. Bubbles were in the bathtub. She almost moaned.

Ray unbuttoned Stella's shirt and removed her bra, pants, and underwear. Stella finished removing his tank top, shoes, and pants. The music was still following them. He got in first and held out his hand to help her in. He sat, and she sat against him. Stella had to ask. "How is the music following us?"

Then Ray pointed to the outlet and the speaker sticking out. "Seb let me borrow his."

"We need to get some because this is awesome," she said. Ray laughed.

Holding her like this after everything they had been through in such a brief period was everything. He closed his eyes and sighed.

"Everything is so beautiful," she said. "The ring is amazing."

He kissed her neck and whispered, "I'm so happy you like it."

Stella whispered, "I love it." He grabbed the soap and slowly started rubbing his hands over her body. She closed her eyes, enjoying the feel of Ray's hands caressing her. She turned around on his lap gently so as not to make the water spill over. They kissed and embraced as if it were the last time. It got hot and heavy fast, and they decided they should get out of the water and take it to the bed. They dried off, and Ray carried her to the bed as if it were their honeymoon. He laid her down slowly. He wanted to take his time and make this night a memorable one.

He hovered over her and looked into her eyes. "I love you so much, Stella."

She traced the outline of his jaw. "I love you more."

He lowered his head and continued to make passionate love to her.

There was no rush. They had forever.

Chapter 47

Three hours later, they were both starving. Stella got up to find the chicken wings and French fries. Ray knew her so well.

She heated up their food, and they sat down for dinner half naked, with nothing but underwear on. It was delicious and hit the spot. "I haven't texted ma yet. It's late out there," Stella said.

"Send it anyway. I bet you she's up," Ray said with his head down, as if he was keeping a secret.

"You told her, didn't you?" Stella said, and Ray laughed.

"Listen, I had to ask permission first!" Stella grabbed her phone, and she had a million messages from Seb and Kay. She sent the pictures to her mom, who immediately called her.

Stella picked up. "Hi, Ma." Ray heard the screaming from the other end of the phone. He smiled.

"Yes, Ma. It was beautiful and perfect. I'm feeling better." More talking on the other side. "Yeah, Ma, I'm good. Never been better," she said, looking at Ray and smiling. "Ok. love you too. He loves you too. *Bendición*. Bye."

Chapter 48

Stella will pay for ruining my life. She walks around like it's nothing, as if she is the utmost high. Thinking she and Ray will walk away with the fame, fortune and the big house. No, they won't. Not if I have anything to say about it. Jason did a good job of almost breaking her two years ago. Bless his heart. He would do anything for me, including getting close to her. As usual, this pest is back again. With her innocent-looking face. She makes me sick to my stomach. Eventually she will be out of the way for good. I wait for the day. I will be on top finally. Jason will just have to come back and finish the job.

Chapter 49

The next three months went by, and things were going great. Seb got his promotion. Kayla was really showing now. She was having a baby girl. Seb was hyped because that baby girl was going to have his green eyes. He was sure of it! Either way, that baby was going to be the most beautiful thing ever. She would need her own "baby of Instagram" account.

Ray still had a month left of voice work on his new movie. Vince had been working on getting Ray's name out there. They were set up to go to a movie premiere tomorrow. He and Stella had fallen into a great rhythm, and she was doing great at work. She had joined a gym to keep herself busy while Ray was at work. Having her with him had done wonders for him, and it boosted her confidence. She hadn't had a nightmare in over a month, which was the longest so far. So in Ray's mind, that was progress.

Stella was nervous about this premiere, but she needed to get used to this. Her man was going to be a star. She had no doubt. Kay came over to help her do her hair and makeup since that wasn't her strong suit. Kay put her hair in an updo. Stella's dress was red. Ray had a black tuxedo with a red tie and kerchief to match her dress. When Stella was done, she stood up and looked in the mirror.

Kay whistled. "You look stunning, Miss Thang." Just then, Ray walked in all dressed up, and they eyed each other. Slow smiles spread across their faces. "Ok, guys, I'm gonna go so you can finish getting ready," Kay said giving them each a hug and kiss before leaving.

Stella got a text message one minute later and checked it. It was Kayla.

Kay: Girl…Ray was looking FINEEEEE! you better get his ass tonight! Stella laughed.

Stella looked at herself in the mirror. This dress was long. Her feet would hurt in these shoes. She was so out of her element. "You look amazing," Ray said, standing behind her and putting his arms around her.

"So do you! Let's go do this," she said, looking at him with a big smile.

They arrived at the premiere and saw tons of photographers taking pictures. Reporters doing interviews. Ray was flying under the radar still, so they didn't expect too much attention. He saw people from the agency there waiting for them, including Vincent. Ray got out of the limo first and helped Stella out.

"Are you ok?" Ray asked, looking into her eyes. Stella looked around. She smiled and nodded. The immense pride she felt for Ray right now was overwhelming.

Ray was busy admiring everything surrounding them, and Stella watched him taking in the moment. It was selfie time. She pulled her phone out, and they took two selfies. They looked like a formidable couple and not just kids from Brooklyn living a dream.

"You two look like something out of a magazine. Looking good!!" Vince said. "This is Bob from PR. He'll be walking you through the red carpet." Ray held on to Stella's hand while they posed for pictures and made their way inside. Stella was amazed by the hoopla. It was beautiful. Everyone was dressed up. She saw the stars of the movie ahead of them.

The lead actress, Lindsay Pollack, saw them in the lobby of the theater and approached them.

"Hi. I'm Lindsay." She was the most beautiful woman Stella had ever seen in person. Ray's height, blond, thin. She was wearing a black dress. There was a gleam in her eyes.

Ray stuck his hand out. "Ray."

Stella followed. "Stella, Ray's fiancée."

"It's nice to meet you both. I also work with Vince. He's fantastic."

"Yes, he's been great," Ray responded. Stella noticed the way this woman was looking at Ray. She was going to need alcohol to get through tonight and probably the rest of her life. He didn't even realize the attention he got.

"It was nice meeting you both. Enjoy the movie," Lindsay said.

Stella replied, "Yes, we will!" She wanted to make sure Lindsay knew Ray was spoken for and she should beat it. Lindsay gave Ray one last look and walked away.

Vince came over, and Stella wanted to give Ray his space.

"I'm going to grab a drink. Do you want anything?" she asked Ray and Vince. They both declined.

Stella walked to the bar and asked for a Coke. Even though she wanted something stronger, she didn't want to embarrass Ray in any way. Just then a tall figure came, stood next to her and ordered a drink. There were no stools so everyone was leaning against the bar. Stella recognized him from the poster as the male lead, Rick Johnson. He was tall, dark, bald. He looked down at Stella and smiled. She gave him a tight smile back.

"Hi, I'm Rick." He stuck his hand out for a handshake.

"Yeah, I know. Your face is plastered everywhere. Stella." She shook his hand with a smile.

He laughed. "You're funny."

"I have my moments," she replied with a crooked smile, and Rick chuckled. The bartender came back with her Coke. She thanked the bartender and left him a little something in the tip jar. She turned and saw Vince and Ray talking to another gentlemen. She would keep her distance until they were done.

"Who are you here with?" Rick asked her.

"Vincent Flemming and my fiancé, Ray Garcia," she said, pointing in their direction.

"Oh, ok, I'm repped by Vince too. It's nice to finally talk to somebody who isn't a reporter and just have a regular conversation. So, Stella, where are you from?" he asked, taking a sip of his drink and looking around the room.

"Brooklyn."

"Ahhh yes. The infamous accent." Stella rolled her eyes, and he laughed. "Hear that a lot?" he asked.

"More than I like," she said with a smile and looking down at her drink.

"That's ok. It gives character. I know Brooklyn."

"Oh yeah? Where are you from?" she asked him.

"Chicago, but I was raised in Red Hook."

"Nice. I was raised in the Gowanus projects."

"So we're neighbors."

"Practically down the block," she said, and they both laughed.

Just then Ray noticed Stella talking to Rick and started walking over to them. Ray's gaze bored into Stella. Stella knew he was jealous.

"Ray, meet Rick. Rick, my fiancé, Ray Garcia." They shook hands, and it felt like a sizing up.

"It's nice to meet you, Ray. You're a lucky guy. She's funny." How long were they talking? Ray thought.

"Nice to meet you too. Yes, I am a lucky guy," he said, looking at Stella and giving her a wink.

"It was nice meeting you both. Stella, it was a pleasure. Enjoy the movie. I'll see you around at Vince's office," Rick said, and he walked off.

Ray looked at Stella, and she looked at him. "You have fun making me jealous, right?" Ray said.

"Absolutely not. I ordered a drink. He ordered a drink and introduced himself. It's not like he was eating me with his eyes like Lindsay was with you," Stella said, rolling her eyes.

"Yeah, well, you didn't see him from where I was standing," Ray said, and he pulled her closer to him. "What are you drinking?"

"A Coke. I didn't want these people to think your fiancée is a lush," she said, and they both laughed. He took a sip from her drink.

"You look stunning, Mr. Garcia."

"You look ravishing, soon-to-be Mrs. Garcia." He gave her a kiss.

Chapter 50

They watched the movie, which ended up being surprisingly good. Everyone stood up and gave a standing ovation for the period piece film. Ray and Stella held hands the entire time. They ran into Rick on the way out. "What did you guys think?" he asked.

"I thought it was great," she said. Stella felt Ray's arm get tighter around her.

Ray replied, "Yeah, it was great."

"Great! I'm glad you both enjoyed it," Rick said, and he ran off with a group of people.

Ray looked at Stella and mimicked "I thought it was great" with a face, and she busted out laughing. Ray's sarcasm was one of the reasons she loved him so much. Their sarcasm together was unmatched. This jealousy thing was turning them both on. They left and got into the limo. There was a partition between the driver and them. Ray grabbed Stella and pulled her onto his lap. He kissed her hard. "You're mine," he growled. She loved when he said that.

"I am yours," she growled back. The ride was too short. They walked in and practically ripped each other's clothes off. Thank God it was a Saturday night. Stella planned to sleep late tomorrow.

After they finished, Stella was hungry. "Babe, are you hungry?"

"Yeah, I could eat again," he said with a smirk. She laughed. Stella went to the fridge and started making sandwiches. Ray's favorite—turkey, American cheese, mayo, lettuce, tomatoes, salt, and pepper. They sat together eating.

"How do you feel?" Stella asked him.

"Like I'm in a dream," he said, taking a bite of his sandwich.

Stella nodded. "Good. You deserve all the good things coming."

"We deserve it," he corrected her.

Stella's tomboy insecurities were nagging her. What if Ray found a girlie girl that he fell in love with, like that Lindsay chick they had met? Stella would always feel as though she wasn't good enough for Ray, but she knew nobody would love him the way she did, and nobody would love her the way he did.

"This sandwich is delicious," he said, breaking the silence. Stella moaned as she took another bite and nodded. It was moments like this they enjoyed the most. Ray had been working long hours, and it was hard. He wouldn't get home until 1:00 a.m. or later, and she would be falling asleep or asleep already a lot of the time when he got home. She always had a plate of food with a note of encouragement waiting for him when he got home. He loved coming home. Those notes were everything, and he kept them all. He made sure to hold her close when he came to bed. She would moan "hi" and say, "I love you." And fall back asleep.

She got up and cleared their plates, washed them, and put them away.

He was off tomorrow for the first time in weeks.

She grabbed his hand. They would take advantage of the time they had.

Chapter 51

The next day Stella got a text from Kayla while she and Ray were in bed. It was a picture of Ray and Stella from last night. Pictures from the premiere were all over the internet.

"Oof, look at that couple. They're smokin'," Ray said of their picture.

Stella's mind started racing. Her face was serious.

"What's wrong?" he asked.

"Nothing. We look good together. Check us out!"

Ray raised an eyebrow but let it go.

They looked like those couples she saw in the tabloids. Beautiful. They had to remain grounded no matter what. Stella had to make sure Ray always remembered where he came from. And her for that matter. If Ray was this hot successful actor and she was his woman, she couldn't lose herself either. But the thought on Stella's mind was that anybody who wanted to could find her now. She couldn't let Ray know that thought was on her mind. There would be tons of premieres and pictures. She couldn't live in fear.

Kay and Seb were coming over for dinner later that day. They arrived at around 4:00 p.m. Kay's belly was growing, and everybody was highly anticipating this baby girl's arrival. She had Jordans in all colors thanks to Titi Stella. Seb and Kay still weren't set on a particular name for her.

"Guys, how did it go last night? You both looked amazing. Is that Rick or whatever his name is as big as he looks in pictures?" Kay asked.

"Yeah, ask Stella about that," Ray sneered from the kitchen, and Stella rolled her eyes.

Kay looked at her with a surprised look.

"It was nothing. I was getting a Coke from the bartender. He came up and ordered a drink. Introduced himself. Ray was busy talking to a gentleman with Vince, so I didn't want to interrupt."

"Uh-huh. Yeah, that's the reason," Ray chimed in. "I look over and these two are just all smiles."

"Ok, so first of all, we weren't all smiles. Second, he asked where I was from, I said Brooklyn, and he said, 'Ahhh yes, the infamous accent.' I laughed, and that's when Ray came over. So sue me!"

"Jealous, were we, Ray?" Seb said from the table.

"See how he leaves out the part before my interaction with Rick, where that lead bitch Lindsay whatever comes over and starts eye fuckin' Ray right in front of me!"

"Nooooo," Kay said, looking at Ray. Seb looked at him, and Ray tried to hold back a laugh.

"She's exaggerating," Ray said with a big smile on his face. Stella shook her head. They all laughed. "It's ok, though, 'cause it all worked out in the end anyway," Ray said, and he winked at Stella.

"Anyways, how are you guys doing? Seb, how's the new job? Kay, how are you feeling?" Stella asked.

"The job is great. The pay is great. I can't complain. Can't wait for my little mama to hurry up and be here," he said, looking lovingly at Kay. Kay was glowing. Being pregnant looked good on her. She looked like a regal queen.

"I'm feeling good. She is kicking the shit out of me constantly, but otherwise I feel great."

"You look great, mama," Stella told Kayla. "We're so excited."

Stella put out a spread of chicken, mashed potatoes, rice, and steak. She knew Kay had a hankering for steak, so she wanted to make sure Kayla enjoyed herself. The guys went out to get beer at the store. Stella finally had Kay to herself.

"Kay, do you think it's possible Jason will come for me if he sees those pictures? I mean, he never contacted me again after that night, but I swear I saw him twice before we left. It could've just been me, but I swear it was him."

"God knows. That motherfucker was crazy. How sure are you that it was him?"

"I'm pretty sure, but like I said, it could've been anybody. I don't even want to mention anything to Ray. We are going to be doing tons of pictures eventually, and I don't want anything to get in the way of his success."

Kayla understood where she was coming from. "How are your nightmares?"

"Haven't had any for a month," Stella said, raising the roof with her hands. They laughed.

"Yeah, that's all that good lovin' you're getting from Ray. He's banging your brains out, so you forget." They busted out laughing. It was the good hearty laugh they needed.

"How are things with Seb?"

"Everything is great. I love him more than anything. He's so happy with his new job. The pay is much better, which is great. The pregnancy sex is…I can't even describe." Kay rolled her eyes just thinking about it. "Better than regular sex, and he can't wait until little mama arrives. Stel, I'm so excited. I got so lucky."

Stella listened intently. "Kay, you and Seb deserve this. You're made for each other." Maybe one day she would know what that felt like when she had a baby of her own on the way.

The guys got back. Stella was in the bedroom, and Kayla was in the bathroom. Ray came running to her. "Seb's going to propose next weekend," he said, whispering, but Puerto Ricans were naturally loud.

"Shhhhhhhh," Stella said, and she ran out to Seb and gave him a quick hug before Kayla came out of the bathroom. Seb and Kay stood for a couple more hours just talking crap and reminiscing.

"Do you guys remember that chick Seb was with the day I met Stella?" Ray asked, and Stella rolled her eyes.

"She was a ditz and a half. It was like watching Rose from *The Golden Girls* in real life," Stella said, and they all laughed.

Seb nodded his head. "I remember meeting Kayla at one of Stella's birthday parties, and she was with that doofus Jack. I hated that guy."

Chapter 52

November 22, 2015—It was Stella's twenty-first birthday, and they were all meeting up at a restaurant. It was before Ray took her to the hotel to be intimate for the first time.

Seb was there already with Cindy. Kayla walked in with Jack; Stella walked over to give her a hug. Seb's eyes opened wide. He said aloud to Ray, "Is that Kayla?"

"Yeah." Ray saw his face and knew his friend was smitten. Stella made the introductions, and when Kay shook Seb's hand, he held onto it for a beat longer. His green eyes were smoldering, and Kayla noticed.

"Seb, this is Jack, Kayla's boyfriend," Stella said, with emphasis on the word *boyfriend*. Seb snapped out of it and shook Jack's hand. Stella noticed that look Seb had, and she saw the way Kayla was looking at him. They sat directly across from each other. Cindy was talking some nonsense. Kayla gave Stella a look like *Who is this?* Seb looked mortified. Cindy was a pretty girl and had a good heart, but it was clear Seb was on another level. Jack was quiet, and Kayla had to drag him into the conversation. Seb stared at him as if to ask, How did you land this goddess?

Kayla pulled Stella to the side the first chance she got her alone. "Seb is fine! You didn't tell me he was that gorgeous. Who is that ditz he's with?"

"That's his girlfriend, Cindy. Poor girl. They don't match at all."

"They don't, and the looks he's giving me with those eyes…Oh my God, I may have to leave Jack." They both giggled.

Jack was good looking in his own way. He was dark skinned, around Kayla's height. Nice build. Glasses. Short hair. He worked at an accountant's office. He was a good guy. But when Kayla saw Seb, she realized what it was like to get hit with the love bug at first sight. There was something there, especially when they shook hands, and he held her hand.

"I want her," Seb told Ray. Ray knew that when Seb said he wanted something he would get it.

"Dude, you're here with Cindy. Just don't disrespect her. It's not nice. Trust me, I get it. But still."

"I know, but Kayla will be mine eventually," Seb said, looking at Kayla from across the room. He loved Kay from the moment he laid eyes on her. If he hadn't been with Cindy, he would've stolen her from Jack. Jack didn't know what to do with all that woman, he thought.

There was a small dance floor in the restaurant. All three couples got on the dance floor with their partners. Seb was dancing with Cindy but was staring at

Kayla. Kayla was dancing with Jack but felt Seb's stare boring into her. She stole glances in his direction, and he smiled at her. She smiled back.

Kayla and Stella started dancing back to back the way they did when they got together, and Seb ended up in front of Kayla. "Hey," he said with a smile.

"Hey yourself," Kayla said, looking to see where Jack and Cindy were.

"I come in peace," Seb said, holding his hands up. "Since those two are our best friends, we should probably get acquainted," he said, and Kayla agreed and shook hands. The hand-holding lasted for several seconds. His eyes were killing her, and he knew it. Just then, Cindy came over.

"Hey, there you are!" she said, and Seb let out a sigh. Kayla laughed and turned around. Jack was a few steps from her.

* * *

Coming back to present, Kay and Seb laughed.

"I can't believe you stood with her all that time," Kay said, rolling her eyes.

"I can't believe you stood with him all that time," Seb said, mimicking her eye roll. "Whether you were in a relationship or not in San Diego, you were going to leave being mine."

Stella fanned herself mockingly. Kayla looked at Seb. "Yeah, I know. Your super sperm made sure of that." They all laughed.

When they left, Stella asked Ray, "Ok, so how's he going to do it?" And he gave her the details.

Chapter 53

By Wednesday, Seb, Stella, and Ray had all the plans down. It was going to be beautiful. After everything Kayla had done for Stella over the past four years, she deserved everything. The man she loved, the beautiful baby girl that was coming, all the happiness in the world. Stella couldn't wait for this weekend.

Stella's boss, Judith Frey, called her into her office after lunch.

"Hey, Stella. We have a law firm from New York City coming in next week Wednesday. I'm supposed to meet with one of the partners and a junior associate. I would like you to be part of the meeting to take notes."

"Sure, no problem. Names and times?"

"The law firm is Morris, Stein, and Manus. We are meeting with Mr. Manus and his associate at 1:00 p.m. I don't have a name for that person yet. The meeting is regarding a merger between our two firms."

"Got it," Stella said, writing down the last note.

"Stella, you've been doing a wonderful job here, and we love having you. The staff loves you, and Melissa was right about you. That's why I'm giving you a raise. I'm bumping you up from $65,000 a year to $75,000 a year." Stella couldn't believe it. Raises weren't normally given without a fight or a negotiation.

"Oh my God, thank you so much. I love working here. Everybody is so nice. I was so nervous about moving out here and having everybody hate me."

"Quite the contrary—we all love you. Keep up the good work."

"I will! Thank you again," Stella said, and she got up.

"Stella, one more thing." Stella turned around.

"I saw you with your fiancé at that movie premiere. Lucky girl. He is fiiiiiine." Judith said fanning herself. Stella laughed.

"Yeah, I am lucky."

Judith smiled, and Stella walked out. She texted Ray right away to tell him about the raise. She was so excited.

* * *

Chapter 54

Saturday was the day.

Stella and Ray were ready. Seb was nervous as hell. Even though he knew she would say yes, the act itself was nerve-wracking. Ray and Stella had helped put this together so quickly. It was a big endeavor, but everybody was on board.

Seb and Kay arrived at the Marina Del Rey. Vincent had let Ray borrow the boat for the night for them to use. Holding Kay's hand, Seb led her onto the boat. There was a table for two in the middle of the room. There were dim lights everywhere. Seb was dressed in white from head to toe. He had on a crisp white suit—like the black one Ray had worn when he proposed to Stella.

He had had Kay wear white as well. She looked stunning in a fitted white dress that curved around her belly like a glove.

"This is beautiful," she said, looking at him. He smiled. They sat down to eat. And the boat started moving as the sun was setting. "Is it just us on this boat?" she asked, and he nodded. He was so nervous. Ray and Stella were nervous too. Kay moaned—the steak and potatoes on her plate were delicious. Steak was her go-to food during her pregnancy.

"This is so good," she said with her eyes closed. She seemed to be savoring everything on her plate.

They finished eating, and Seb stood up. He led her over to the window so they could see the sun setting. They were surrounded by dim light now. Sebastian took a step back as Keith Sweat's "I'll Give All My Love to You" started playing in the background. As he took a step back, everyone took a step forward. Stella, Ray, Sandra, and Kay's parents—her mom, Patricia, and her dad, Gregory. All wearing white. Kayla turned around and saw all those familiar faces behind Seb, who was down on one knee with the ring box opened in his hand.

"My queen. From the moment I met you, I knew we were destined for this. Even if it took us seven years and a daughter on the way to get here, there's no doubt that us meeting in San Diego was fate."

Kayla's tears were falling, and so were everybody else's. Stella was standing in front of Ray and holding Patricia's hand.

Seb continued, "I want to spend the rest of my life with you. Kay, will you be my wife?"

Kayla choked out a yes. Seb slipped the ring onto her finger, moved forward to kiss her stomach, and got up to give her a hug and a kiss. The photographer got some great shots. Kayla had no idea the photographer was even there the whole time.

She finally got a chance to look around and lost it when she saw her mom. They cried in each other's arms. Gregory gave Seb a big hug and handshake.

Kayla gave Stella the biggest hug. They cried together, knowing everything they had been through. Well, mostly Stella, and without Kayla she knew she would not have been able to get through any of it.

Stella went to hug Seb. He gave her a big hug. "Thank you for having her as a friend. Thank you for all your help setting this up."

Stella looked at him. "Don't thank me. Thank Ray for all of it. For being in Coney Island that day. For choosing me." Stella's heart was so full for her friends. Well, they were family. She couldn't call them friends anymore. As far as she was concerned, she had her brother and sister and a niece on the way.

Patricia approached, and Stella let her have her moment with her new soon-to-be son-in-law.

Ray walked up to Stella and wrapped his arms around her. He gave her a kiss.

"We did good," he said, looking around.

"Yeah, we did. It's beautiful." She looked around too.

Sandra walked up to them. "Everything is so pretty. You guys are something else," she said, smiling. "Ray, is it ok if I steal my daughter for a sec?"

He kissed Stella's head and released her. "Of course." Stella was on the fence and telling him with her eyes not to leave.

Sandra turned to Stella. This was the first time she had seen her since she left. "How are you feeling, Stel?"

"I feel great, Ma. To be honest, the best I've ever been. Work is great. Ray is great. Kay and Seb are great." And that was the truth. Stella was the happiest she had ever been. "The doctor said I'm ok and we can try to have kids whenever we want."

"Any nightmares?" Sandra asked, concerned.

"Not in a month. It's like my mind knows I'm safe with Ray."

"Have you been eating and taking care of yourself?"

"Yup. I joined a gym here. We don't eat out much. I try to cook every day so Ray can take food with him since he doesn't get home until late, and I don't want him eating out every day."

"That's good. I'm so happy for you, Stella. You're doing amazing. Better than I could ever have hoped for. I'm sorry I wasn't here when you needed me. I was going to jump on a plane and come, but Ray said you were safe."

Stella nodded. "Yes, I was. Ray was a trooper, and Kay and Seb were there too. Plus I have a great doctor. So I had a good support system." Sandra gave her a hug.

The photographer started taking pictures of the engaged couple with everyone there.

The boat docked after two hours. Sandra went home with Stella and Ray. Kayla's parents were staying at a hotel nearby as they did not want to intrude on the newly engaged couple, who would want their privacy. Kayla texted Stella later that evening after they got home.

Kay: Thank you for helping Seb with tonight. It was amazing.

Stella: np. It was my pleasure and the least I can do for my sister who's been there for me through allllll the bullshit. I love you both.

What a great night, Stella thought. Since her mom was staying with them, they had to have respect and try not to get frisky.

That would be hard.

Chapter 55

It had been nice coming home to a cooked meal the past couple of days, but Stella's mom had left on a red-eye Tuesday night. Ray got home late that evening, and Stella was already asleep.

Stella was getting ready the following morning and she watched Ray sleep. He looked so at peace. She gave him a kiss on the lips lightly so as not to wake him before she walked out. She locked the door and stepped outside. She walked over to the mailbox to see whether there was anything important. Bills, bills, bills, she thought, and then she came across a single sheet of paper. What the hell is this? she thought.

The paper said, *I see you, Stella.*

She looked around but didn't see anybody. Stella didn't know what this was, but she stuffed it in her purse and went to work. She would not bring this up with Ray.

The morning went fast. Stella was busy getting ready for their guests.

At 12:55 p.m., she got a call from the receptionist, Katie.

"Hey, Stella. Mr. Manus is here with his associate. And girl, the associate is hot!!!" she said, and Stella laughed.

"Ok, I'll let Judith know." Stella called Judith and let her know their guests had arrived.

"Great. Please have Katie take them into conference room A." Judith instructed. Stella called Katie back and gave her the instructions. She waited for Judith to be ready so they could walk in together.

Judith had her game face on when she opened her door. She looked at Stella and said, "Let's do this." Stella nodded.

Chapter 56

They walked into conference room A, and it felt as if the air had been sucked out of the room. Stella saw him and he smiled. Judith noticed Stella's face. She was pale as if she had just seen a ghost. Jason stood up slowly with a smirk on his face, his eyes boring into Stella. Stella felt as if she couldn't move. The room felt like it was closing in on her. Then out of the corner of her eye, she saw Judith and Mr. Manus looking at her. She snapped out of it and had to continue as if nothing had happened. She introduced herself and shook their hands. Jason held on to her hand for longer than necessary. Stella wanted to run, but she couldn't. Judith saw the interaction.

Stella sat and kept her head down for most of the meeting. Every time she looked up, he was staring at her. The face that haunted her dreams for the last two and a half years was mere steps away from her. The meeting felt like forever.

Finally, Judith stood up and asked Stella to escort the guests to the elevators. Just kill me, she thought. "Right this way," she said, leading the way and walking briskly down the hallway to the elevators.

When the elevator rang, Mr. Manus said, "Thank you, Stella." And he shook her hand.

Jason followed, and she had no choice but to shake his hand. When he grabbed her hand tight, he leaned down and whispered in her ear with a smile, "I've been dreaming about how you felt for two years. Can't wait to feel it again." Stella closed her eyes tight. He let her hand go and got on the elevator.

Stella released the breath she had been holding and ran to the bathroom. She would not cry here. She was done crying. She looked at herself in the mirror. She hated this. Apparently, Jason was not going to go away so easily. She was going to have to deal with him eventually so that she could move on 100 percent with her life.

She went back to her desk, and Judith called her into her office. Uh-oh, she thought.

Stella walked in, and Judith said, "Close the door."

She closed the door and sat down.

"Spill it. What's the deal with you and the junior associate?" Stella was not ready for anybody to know her truth here. It was too soon.

Judith was a no-nonsense woman. She was African American, in her late forties, five foot six, with black hair and brown eyes. She wouldn't take anyone's shit. Stella loved and admired her.

"He's just someone I know from Brooklyn. We had one date two years ago that didn't go well." That was somewhat the truth. Judith could read anybody.

"Stella. How unwell did the date go?" Judith asked, sitting up in the chair.

Stella looked her in the eyes and hoped she could read what she was trying to say. "Unwell enough that I had to work from home for two weeks."

From the look on her face, Judith was not expecting that answer. Her eyes softened, and she nodded with understanding. "Get me those notes as soon as you can." That was Stella's cue to leave.

Stella nodded and got up. She left and closed the door behind her. Judith grabbed the phone and called Melissa. "Hey, Mel, it's Judy."

"Hey, girl, how's everything? Is everything ok with Stella?" Melissa asked, sounding concerned.

"Actually, that's why I'm calling. Do you remember her needing to work from home for two weeks a couple of years ago?"

"Oh my God, yes. When she got back, she had this new scar above her eyebrow and there was something going on with her rib cage. I thought she had gotten in a fight, but I didn't want to pry. Why do you ask?"

"Because I think the piece of shit that did that to her was just in my office. I had a meeting with Manus from Morris, Stein, and Manus. This guy was the junior associate. Her face went pale when she saw him, and it's like she froze. I'm not sure if she's in trouble or not. Her boyfriend is a big guy, and I'm sure he can protect her, but this associate had this weird look. He just stared at her the whole meeting, and she kept her head down, like not wanting to look at him."

"That's dicey. Stella is smart. I'm sure she can manage whatever it is."

"Well, she obviously couldn't last time. I'll just do my due diligence on this guy and see what the deal is. Let me let you go, Mel. I'm sure you're busy. Thanks for the info."

"No problem. She's a good kid, Jude. Whatever is going on is not her doing. We'll talk soon." And they hung up.

Judith knew Stella was a good kid. She was the hardest worker she had at the firm. She had proved that in the short time she was there. Being a criminal defense lawyer was difficult, and having good people around helped make the job a little easier.

Chapter 57

Stella got home that night and sat on the sofa. Brandy came and jumped up onto her lap.

"Hey, girl. Were you good today?" Her phone pinged.

Ray: Babe, they moved up the release for Penny's Mission to Christmas 2023 That was great news. It was a family film with dogs, so it would do great for the holiday.

Stella: Omg that's awesome! Hollywood here we come!! Lol

She was nervous about the letter and seeing Jason. This was a problem, and she needed to figure out how to handle it. Hopefully, he had gone back home. She had heard Mr. Manus say they were heading back on a red-eye tonight. So hopefully she would be in the clear. She went to check the mail just in case there were any more letters. She opened the mailbox, and sure enough there was another piece of paper folded up. She ran back inside and opened it.

Did you think moving across the country would keep me away? It was great seeing you, and I can't wait to feel you again. There's nothing your boyfriend will be able to do about it.

Stella was angry. How did he find her? What was going on?

The real question was, should she tell Ray? Yes, of course. He had to know just in case Jason went after him too.

Stella was feeling queasy after dealing with Jason today. She felt nauseated and started thinking about when her last period was. She was having cramps as usual, but she wasn't bleeding. She checked her app. She was two days late. Nothing crazy. Her cycle was probably just off. She hadn't really eaten much today either, so she started cooking.

How would she tell Ray she had seen her rapist today and he had promised to do it again? She didn't think she had a choice but to go to the police. Again, she didn't know what good that would do because if he wanted to get to her, he would, and there was nothing they could do, or it would be too late.

Chapter 58

Ray got home at 1:00 a.m., his usual time, but Stella was wide awake, sitting on the sofa with Brandy. Brandy went nuts when she saw him. He picked her up. Stella got up to give him a kiss. "Hi, ma," he said. "What are you doing up?"

"Come sit."

"What happened?" His face changed completely. He sat with her, and she had the letters on the table.

"This was in the mail this morning when I left." And she showed him the first letter. She saw his jaw tighten. She blew a breath out and continued, "The junior associate that was with Mr. Manus today…was Jason."

Ray stood up. He didn't even know what to do with himself. "What happened?" he asked through his teeth as he sat back down.

"Judith and I walked in, and I froze. He smiled because he had gotten the reaction he wanted. But I had to snap out of it because I didn't want to embarrass her. I shook their hands, and he had this grin on his face when he grabbed my hand. Judith noticed everything because she called me into her office after it was over. The meeting lasted for what felt like forever. I kept my head down and took the notes. Every time

I looked up, he was staring at me." Stella was fighting tears now, and Ray sat back down and took her hand. She continued. "Judith asked me to walk them to the elevator, and right before he got on, he leaned down and whispered so only I could hear him, and I quote, 'I've been dreaming about how you felt for two years. Can't wait to feel it again.'"

Ray stood up again. "I'm going to kill that ballsy motherfucker." He was livid, and Stella knew how Ray could fly off the handle. If she could have avoided telling him, she would have, but she had to for his own safety.

"There's more," she said, and he looked down at her. "When I got home, there was another letter in the mail." She handed him the second letter. Ray couldn't see straight after reading it. His blood was boiling.

"I think we have to go to the police," she said. "I don't have just myself to worry about now. It was different before, but now we have people and careers we must protect." She grabbed his hand. "Ray, I need you to hear what I'm saying." He looked at her, and his anger was palpable. "We cannot jeopardize you or your career for this. We have to be smarter than that. I think we go to the police tonight to make them aware. And we must let Vince know because his job is to protect you, and he will know what to do."

Ray didn't want to fight with her after the day she had had. "Ok. Let's go to the police first thing in the morning." He was exhausted and angry and not in the right frame of mind. She nodded.

"You hungry, babe?"

"Yeah, ma." He ate, and they tried to fall asleep. Except this night, Jason's face was back in Stella's dreams.

Chapter 59

They woke up the next morning and got ready. Stella would head to work right after and so would Ray. Stella texted Judith to let her know she would be a little late and Judith said ok. Ray called Vince to let him know what was going on. He held her hand tight as they walked into the police station. They asked to speak to someone about a possible stalking situation and were escorted to a room.

A detective walked in and introduced himself. "I'm Detective James Sharpe," he said, and he shook their hands. He was massive—at least six foot, with a weight in the two hundreds—African American, and in his late thirties or early forties. It was like LA was where all the good-looking people were, Stella thought.

"I'm Ray Garcia, and this is my fiancée, Stella Gomez."

"It's nice to meet you both. How can I help you?" he asked, and Stella started telling him everything that had happened, even showing him the pictures of what Jason had done to her.

Sharpe had a look on his face as if he wanted to kill the guy that had done this. "I'm so sorry," he said, and she continued telling him about how she got the first letter, he showed up to her job, and then she received the second letter.

"This guy is ballsy," Sharpe said.

"Those were the exact words I used," Ray said.

"Stella, I need you to fill out some forms explaining everything you told me. We will put a restraining order in place so that he stays away from you both. If he tries to get near you, he will be arrested."

To Stella, all that was nonsense. They wouldn't be able to do anything. This was all a formality so it would look as if they had done everything they could to take care of the situation. She and Ray filled out the paperwork and handed it to detective Sharpe.

"Hey, Stella. I'm sorry about what happened to you. Trust me, if he comes back, I'm going to get his ass. I hate guys like him. Smug. My family is all women, so I take this personally." They all shook hands.

"Thanks for your time," Ray said, and they walked out.

"We need to let Seb and Kay know too, just in case," Stella said.

"Seb knows already. He's ready for anything." Stella was pissed that her friends were mixed up in all this. She was feeling nauseous again. She hadn't eaten much yesterday, and she hadn't had breakfast yet.

"Babe, please stop at McDonald's so I can grab something. I'm starving." In the back of her mind, today was day three. Her period still hadn't come. She would take a test when she got home just to make sure. She got to work and let Judith know she was there.

"Everything ok, Stel?" Judith asked with a concerned look on her face.

Stella had to be open with this woman. Unfortunately, circumstances right now were such that everyone in her life had to know what was going on, even if she didn't want to talk about it.

"Do you have a second to talk?" Stella asked. Judith quickly nodded.

Stella closed the door, sat down, and started talking. It got easier every time she told the story, meaning Jason didn't hold much over her anymore.

"The junior associate from yesterday, Jason Guerrero. We went on a date two years ago. When I rejected his kiss, he beat and raped me. I received a letter in the mail yesterday morning when I left my house, but I didn't think anything of it. Then he showed up here, and when I got home, there was another letter." Judith listened. "Ray and I went to the police station this morning to take out a restraining order on him so that he can't come anywhere near us."

"You did the right thing. I was a personal witness to his smug ass. The way he stared at you the whole meeting was unnerving, and I knew there was something going on." She paused. "Thank you for sharing that. I know something like that is extremely personal and difficult to share. I will make sure they never come back here. I don't know if Manus knows the piece of shit he has working for him, but I'm sure he'll find out soon."

Stella got up and was about to leave.

"Hey, Stel…"

"Yeah?"

"If you or Ray ever needs a defense attorney, I got you both," Judith said with an eyebrow raised.

"Thanks." Stella smiled and walked out.

Chapter 60

Stella was being extra vigilant, and Ray was texting her every chance he could to make sure she was ok. Stella texted Kay.

Stella: Hey mama.

Kay: Girlll what in the batshit craziness is going on?? Seb is losing it over here.

It was too much to text. She called and gave Kay the rundown of what had happened.

Stella got home and tentatively checked the mail. Scared of what she would find. She let out a sigh of relief when the mailbox was empty. She opened her door, and there was a letter stuck in the door. Oh no! she thought. Brandy greeted her, and she was relieved Brandy was ok. She read the letter.

The cops won't be able to save you.

Tell Stella something she didn't know. She texted Ray a pic of the letter and then called Detective Sharpe. He told her to put it in a plastic bag. They wanted to try to get prints off it. Meanwhile, they needed to get out of that apartment for the time being. Ray called her to make sure she was ok. Stella checked the apartment just in case. There was nothing else out of place, no other letters. She called Ray and said, "Ray, we can't stay here."

"I know, ma. We'll figure something out tonight when I get home." She said ok and hung up.

Meanwhile, she had one more thing to clear up for peace of mind. She went to the bathroom and peed on the stick. After five minutes, she looked at it and thought, "Yup…sounds about right."

Ray got home, and Stella was awake. They were awake a lot now. They might as well get used to no sleep, she thought. "Hi, ma," he said. "You ok?" She nodded with a smile and handed him a small narrow gift box.

"You got me a gift with all this shit going on?" he said, smiling.

"Well, technically you got us a gift," she said, and he opened it. There were two positive tests in it. His eyes opened wide. "For real?" he whispered, and she nodded her head yes with a big smile. He grabbed her and kissed her. Then reality hit. They had a third person to protect now.

She saw the realization in his face. "We have to protect this baby at all costs, pa," she said, and he nodded, but he just wanted to enjoy this before reality hit tomorrow.

"Can't believe it," he said, smiling and touching her stomach. He dropped to his knees and talked to his peanut. "Nothing is ever going to happen to you or your mom. I promise," he said, and he kissed Stella's stomach. Stella held him close to her.

Chapter 61

A week later Stella got a call from Detective Sharpe advising her that the restraining order had been executed and served to Jason in New York. They initially had a hard time finding him. Apparently, he was good at going under the radar for some reason. But they finally tracked him down and served him.

Meanwhile, Ray and Stella were staying at an apartment Vince owned. Vince understood what was going on, since he had had clients who had stalkers before. Ray and Stella were good people, and he wanted to help them. They had a strong support system that was ready to go head to head with whatever Jason threw at them. Little did they know he had help on this side of the country.

Stella had an appointment with Dr. Sawyer and she and Ray were so excited.

Dr. Sawyer walked in with a big smile. "Ok, Stella, let's see what's going on here." She looked over her paperwork. They had had Stella pee in a cup before the doctor came in.

"It's definitely positive," she said. "Shall we try to find him or her?" Ray and Stella looked at each other and nodded. Stella lay down. Dr. Sawyer put the jelly on her stomach and began doing the sonogram. She found the baby fast. And they saw it on the screen. This little person.

"Peanut," Ray said quietly. Stella cried. This moment was everything to her.

"Your tentative due date is November 1."

"A Scorpio," Stella said quietly to herself. Scorpios were tough, she thought. Puerto Ricans were big on horoscopes. She remembered her mother watching Walter Mercado when she was little and taking those horoscopes to heart.

Dr. Sawyer continued, "Stella, you have to try to take it easy so we can ensure a smooth nine months." Easier said than done, Stella thought, and she looked at Ray. He knew what she was thinking. The images were printed out and given to them. They were amazed. Now that it was official, they could tell Seb and Kay.

Ray took a picture of the sonogram and sent it to the group chat when they left. But they were the only ones that would know. Everybody else would have to wait a little while longer.

Kay: OMG! Congratulations!

Seb: Holy Shit! Congrats!!

Ray and Stella hugged. What a blessing, they thought.

Kay: Our kids can play together

Kayla was due April 3.

Stella sent a message separately to Kay:

Stella: Kay, the baby is due Nov 1

Kay: Sis, I'm so excited for you and Ray. After everything you've been through and continue to go through because of Jason, you manage to have a successful job, with the second most perfect guy at the perfect time." Stella laughed. Kay continued.

Kay: I wish you and Ray nothing but the best. Hopefully, we can end this shit with Jason fast so we can just be pregnant in peace. Jesus.

Exactly what Stella thought. What did Jason want two years later? Why was he doing this now and across the damn country? What were his motives? Stella could not figure it out for the life of her.

Ray dropped Stella off at work and said, "I still can't believe it."

"I can't either. It's surreal right now. Let's celebrate tonight," she said with a smile. Brandy is going to be a big sister."

Ray smiled. "Yes, she is."

They kissed, and he held her there. "I love you, Stel," he said in a low voice.

"I love you too, Ray."

He touched her stomach and said, "My little peanut." Stella nodded.

"Yup. That's your little peanut," she said, smiling.

Chapter 62

Stella walked into the office on cloud nine. She sat down and started going through the mail. There was one envelope not addressed. With a raised eyebrow, she opened it.

Did you Really think you could avoid me? Ha ha. Here I am. In your hands, and you with a panicked look on your face just like when you saw me. Poor Stella. Always poor Stella.

Stella looked for the postmark, and there was none. As if it had been hand delivered. How?

Again, she texted Ray and called Detective Sharpe. She didn't have a plastic bag to put the letter in this time, so Detective Sharpe was coming to get it from her at the office.

Detective Sharpe came in and asked for Stella. Stella saw him walking toward her, and she thought, Man, he's good looking. He came to her and gave her a hug. At this point, they felt like family. Judith came out of her office at the same time and saw him. She must have had the same thought Stella had had because she paused and asked Stella who he was.

Stella made the introduction. "Detective James Sharpe, please meet my boss, Ms. Judith Frey." They shook hands and looked at each other.

"It's nice to meet you, Detective Sharpe."

"Likewise, Ms. Frey," he said with a seductive look. He was really good looking. Judith obviously noticed.

"Stella, you have that thing for me?" Stella nodded and gave him the paper. He put a glove on and took the sheet from her, placing it in his own plastic bag.

Judith watched.

"Stel, did you get a letter here too?" she asked, and Stella nodded.

"Yes, Ms. Frey. That's why I had to call Detective Sharpe," Stella explained.

Judith nodded. "If you need anything, please let me know," Judith said, giving James her card. He nodded at her, and she walked away with a swish to her hips. James looked at Stella and mouthed, "Wow." Stella smiled and giggled under her breath.

* * *

"Hey Ray, it's been a long time. I know I left you in San Diego, but I was so jealous. I'm over it. Do you want to try again?" Ray read the text from Meghan incredulously.

He looked at it and said, "Not today, Satan!" He deleted it and blocked her number. Fuck out of here, he thought. She must've seen the pictures of him and Stella online.

He had so much going on in his mind. Work, Stella, Jason, the baby. It was a lot. But he was so ready.

He wanted Jason to show his face to him. He would give up his whole career just to put his hands on him once. But he knew Stella would never let him do that. So he just bided his time. He knew it would come. He went to the gym every day before work and was ready.

* * *

This bitch. Pulled a restraining order on Jason. How dare she? It's not like it would stop Jason; it's just the principle. She is going to pay. Soon. I can't believe these morons haven't put two and two together yet. How Jason is related to me, how I got the mail into the mailbox. This is pathetic. And fun. It will all come to a head soon enough.

Chapter 63

It was Saturday. Since he was off today, Stella got up early and started making breakfast for Ray. She spent most of the night thinking about Jason and the person sending the letters. What was the connection? She shook her head. All she wanted to do today was enjoy her day with Ray and Brandy.

"Babe, I was thinking," she said, putting Ray's plate in front of him.

"What's up, ma? These smell delicious," Ray said, inhaling the plate she put in front of him. He had pancakes, bacon, french toast, and hash browns.

"Let's stay home and watch some old movies today. I've been dying to see *The Last Dragon* again. I haven't seen it in a long while. I just want to forget about everything for today," she said with a shrug.

Ray smiled. In his best Sho'nuff voice he said "Who's the master?" and they both laughed. There was nothing like a good 80's movie. "That sounds like a plan," he said, eating a piece of bacon. She started devouring her breakfast. Ray was across from her and watched her. He smiled at her, and she stopped moving with a piece of bacon hanging out of her mouth. He pulled out his phone and took a quick picture of her face. They both started laughing. "The baby is hungry. You have to see your face."

Stella hung her head. "I'm starving and eating for two. It is what it is," she said with a shrug and finished her last bite.

"I gotta be careful. You may eat me," Ray said and gave her a wink.

Looking at him under her eyelashes, "Yeah, I'm going to eat you alright," she said in a breathy tone. Ray smiled and got up to put their dishes in the sink. Stella watched him walk in his pajama bottoms which were hanging low on his hips. Walking back over to her, Ray took her hand so she would stand with him. He gently brushed his lips against hers and moaned.

"*Te quiero mucho,* my Stella," he whispered in a husky voice.

Her eyes still closed, she replied, "I love you too, Ray," in barely a whisper. They held each other in an embrace, and they knew that whatever came next, they would get through it together.

They finished eating and went to sit on the sofa. Ray grabbed the remote and started looking for the movie. Stella grabbed her phone to check her Instagram account to see if her mom had posted any new pictures with her boyfriend. Stella wasn't too fond of social media but she had it just in case. She started following Ray's account a couple of weeks ago for support. He only used it for promotional purposes and he hardly ever went into the app either. He had about 3000 followers. Stella was about to close the app when the friend suggestions popped up. She looked at the second name—Amanda Garcia. It was Ray's ex-wife coming up as a suggestion because apparently Amanda was following Ray's account. Stella looked closer at the thumbnail photo and gasped.

Ray turned to her and asked "What happened?" Stella couldn't speak. He sat back so that he could see what she was looking at. "Is that Amanda?" he asked and Stella nodded. In the thumbnail, it was a picture of Amanda and Jason together. Stella closed her eyes, blew out a breath, opened her eyes again and clicked on Amanda's account. A family picture. Jason and Amanda standing together smiling. The caption said, "Happy Birthday to Me and my twin brother, Jason. Love you, bro."

There it was. It was the connection Ray and Stella were searching for. No wonder she looked so familiar. Stella looked over at Ray, who had his hand covering his mouth.

"Ray, you didn't know?" She asked him incredulously.

"Ma, we weren't together long, and he was never around. They said he was in New York, and they called him JJ. They never said Jason. I can't believe this. Her last name was Rodriguez, not Guerrero. Maybe she was using her mother's last name or something."

Stella started thinking it all through. She gasped. Clarity hit her. "Ray, when did you break up with her?"

"It was around August." He said, and Stella closed her eyes. "Why?"

"Jason started messaging me in September," Stella said and looked at Ray with watery eyes.

"It's my fault," Ray whispered, staring at her with regret. "She set this whole shit up after we broke up. But she made it seem like everything was ok. It doesn't make sense."

"Ray, it's not your fault. You didn't know she was psychotic. A woman scorned is dangerous. Do you know how evil you must be to send your brother after your husband's ex-girlfriend?" Stella shook her head. The reality of something that happened 3000 miles away affected her was beyond comprehension.

"Ok. So now we know. Now what?" Ray asked.

Stella thought for a few seconds and said, "We need proof. I have an idea."

* * *

Ray didn't want to see Amanda's face, but Detective Sharpe agreed with Stella's plan. Ray went back to their apartment alone every night for a week straight. Without Stella.

Jason and Amanda knew the cops were aware of somebody harassing Stella. So she and Ray devised a plan to make it look like they broke up just in case they were outside watching.

He texted Amanda, saying he and Stella had broken up and needed someone to talk to. Her response was swift

Amanda: I'll be right there

He told her to meet him at their apartment. She arrived within twenty minutes, and Stella saw her from the car with Detective Sharpe. They were listening through the surveillance cameras Ray had set up the day before. Seeing Amanda going to meet Ray wearing a crop top and her boobs almost coming out had Stella on the edge of her seat, and she had to refrain from running to chase her down.

Stella also saw another figure after she went inside. "Is that Jason?" Sharpe asked her.

She squinted. "Yes. What the hell?" she said, looking at him.

"Hey, Ray," Amanda said, walking into the apartment and kissing Ray on the cheek. She revolted him, but he had no choice but to play along. She sat on the sofa, and he sat next to her. His phone was nearby facedown, just in case he needed to grab it. "How's everything?"

He sighed and blew out a breath. "Hanging in there. Like I said on the phone, Stella and I broke up.

I know you probably don't care after what happened between us, but I just needed someone to talk to."

Amanda put her hand on his forearm and looked at him with what she thought was a comforting smile. Unfortunately, he kept thinking about gagging in her face. "I'm here for you, Ray. Just because we aren't together, doesn't mean we can't be friends," she said and scooted closer to him.

"Thanks, I appreciate it. I just thought everything was going so well, you know? She opened up and told me something very personal happened to her two years ago." Ray said, and he noticed her shift. She crossed one leg over the other and folded her hands on her knee. Her eyebrow went up, and she said with almost a smirk on her face

"Oh really? What happened?" Was this bitch smirking right now, thinking about what happened to Stella?

"She told me she went on a date a couple of years ago, and the guy got violent with her," Ray said, and his jaw clenched.

"Violent, how?" Ray's eyebrow went up. She wants details. How sadistic could she be? His judgment must have been impaired when he decided to date and eventually marry her. He never got inebriated without Seb ever again. It was the one time he decided to go out with coworkers and they were basically pushing him on top of Amanda.

"She rejected his advances, and then he beat and raped her."

"Oh my goodness. That's awful." But the empathy from her mouth was not translating on her face. "This is why you can never do online dating. There are all kinds of crazy people out there." Ray looked at her and stood up.

"I never said how she met him, Amanda. How did you know she met him online?" he said, and she seemingly realized her mistake.

Amanda stood up. "Enough of this charade. I loved you, Ray. I would have done anything for you. But you always chose her. Every minute we were together, she was occupying your thoughts. You called out her name even when we made love, and I still stood with you." She was crying now. "We were so good together, Ray, and we still can be." She pleaded and reached for him, but Ray took a few steps away.

"Let me get this straight. What you're saying is, you told your brother what happened between us and you sent him to hurt Stella?"

"I created his profile, and I messaged her. I don't know what you see in her. She's pretty plain to me. My brother would do anything for me. I didn't realize how far he would go, but it sounded as if she was hurt physically, the same way you hurt me emotionally. So that was satisfying." The tears she had a few seconds ago were gone.

Stella and Detective Sharpe watched the feed, and Stella felt her tears come down. How could anybody wish that kind of harm on another human? Sharpe gently touched her arm as an offer of support through listening to this craziness. The nightmares. The pain. Speculating about it was one thing, but hearing it confirmed was painful.

Through her tears, Stella saw Jason walking up the five steps into the building. She wiped her tears away quickly.

"We have to go in there now!" She yelled.

Ray couldn't look at Amanda anymore and opened the door to the apartment for her to get out. But, instead, he was met with Jason's fist. Caught off guard, Ray stumbled back, and Jason pounced, knowing that if given a chance, Ray would give him a fight. Jason did not know that Ray loved to fight, and he had the person in front of him that hurt the love of his life.

"That's for hurting my sister," he heard Jason say as he felt a blow. There were sounds of sirens in the background.

Ray shook that hit off and ran to tackle Jason. He fell on top of Jason and with Ray on top, Jason had no chance. Ray swung and gave him a hard shot to the ribs, and he heard a crack. "That's for hurting Stella," Ray yelled. Amanda started screaming for Ray to get off her brother and was trying to pull him off. The door swung open and Detective Sharpe ran in to pull Ray off Jason. Before anyone could stop her, Stella ran in and pulled Amanda by the hair and punched her dead in the face, knocking Amanda on her ass. Another officer came in and grabbed Amanda before she could get at Stella. Handcuffs were placed on both and they were taken away. Stella didn't want to risk hurting the baby, but she deserved to get in that one hit on the person who caused the trauma that affected Stella almost every night for two and a half years.

Ray was bleeding himself from the hits he got from Jason. Stella ran to his side, and he hugged her. She looked up at him through tears. "Are you ok?" she asked with a shaky voice.

He nodded. "Yea, ma. I'm fine. This is nothing," he gestured at the cut above his eye, which was bleeding. "He got me with one good shot because I wasn't expecting him to be behind the door."

Stella wrapped her arms around Ray's waist and cried. It was over. Detective Sharpe came over to Ray and Stella.

"Thank you," Stella said, giving Sharpe a big hug. He hugged her back.

"It was my pleasure," he stated and gave Ray a handshake. Detective Sharpe walked away, but he stopped and turned around, "Hey, Stella?"

"Yeah?" She said, turning to him.

"That boss of yours. Is she seeing anyone?" He asked with a crooked smile.

"Nope. She's very single," Stella grinned and winked at him.

He nodded and walked away.

Chapter 64
One year later

Stella and Kayla looked in the mirror. Today was the day. After the drama, the babies, and everything else in between, they were finally getting married today. It was a frantic race to get back in shape after having the babies, but they had pulled it off and were almost back to their original sizes.

Kayla had little Corina Estella Huerta on her actual due date, April 3. Corina had green eyes just like her daddy but was dark just like her momma. Seb was in love. She was perfect.

Stella had little Ruben Sebastian Garcia on November 3. He looked just like his daddy right down to the smile.

Kayla and Stella had already said the kids would marry each other when they got older. The guys were adamant that they were brother and sister! No incest here. The girls would laugh. Seb didn't want to think that far in the future. His little girl was always going to be his little girl, and any guy that tried to date her would die. It was simple in his mind, really. The kids were in the church with Patricia, Kayla's mom, and Maria, Ray's mom. They sat together.

Stella would be walked down the aisle by Sandra, and Kayla would be walked down the aisle by Gregory. All four of them together as a unit.

It was time. They were each other's maids of honor and best men, so there was no need to have anybody else in the wedding party. The music started, and Brandy, holding the rings, ran down the aisle into Ray's arms. Everybody laughed. The girls started their walk down the aisle. Ray and Seb lost their breath when they saw them.

Kayla and Stella bit their lips when they saw their men standing up at the altar, waiting for them. They would be pregnant again in no time, they thought.

Stella had a simple, form-fitted, sleeveless and strapless white dress with a veil covering her face. Kayla had on a white form-fitted backless dress with a long train and her veil covering her face.

They approached the front. Gregory shook Seb's hand. He then proceeded to give Kayla's hand to Seb. Seb pulled her veil back. He smiled at her, and she smiled back. Ray grabbed Stella's hand from Sandra after giving Sandra a kiss on the cheek. He pulled Stella's veil back and mouthed "Wow" at her. She blushed.

Both couples stood in front of the priest and listened to his words about coming together and the battle that each couple would face. If he only knew the battles they had already faced. They were all war tested. It was time for the vows.

Kayla started reading her vows. "Sebastian. The man of my dreams. The father of our little queen. There's nobody else I could imagine myself standing here with. Me and little mama can't wait to spend the rest of our lives with you. I promise to love and take care of you until my dying breath." She mouthed, "I love you, Seb."

"Kayla. My queen. What a whirlwind it has been. I'm so grateful you came to Comic-Con. It changed our lives. I never would've imagined having you and my little mama in my life. I love you both so much, and I promise to take care of you both until the day I die."

"Ray. Love of my life. Seb is right. It has been a whirlwind." Stella's tears started coming down, but she continued, "You have changed me; you have loved me and our little man. There was never anybody else that I was meant to be with. I love you so much, and I promise to take care of you and Ruben for the rest of my life." Ray wiped away her tears.

"Stella," Ray started, and he put Stella's hand over his heart. "If there were a way for me to express how much I love you more than I already try to, I would. My life felt like it was over when I left New York. God knew we needed each other and brought us back together. Fate. And I promise to love and protect you and my son for the rest of my breathing days." Stella couldn't control the tears. What a sap she was turning into, she thought.

The priest instructed them to grab their rings and had the girls repeat after him first.

"Stella and Kayla, do you both take Ray and Sebastian to be your lawfully wedded husbands. To have and to hold in sickness and in health, as long as you both shall live?"

Stella and Kayla both said, "I definitely do," and they slipped the rings on their men's fingers.

The priest repeated the same for Ray and Seb, and they both said, "I do."

"By the power vested in me, I now pronounce you husbands and wives. You may kiss your brides."

"Finally!" Seb exclaimed. And everybody laughed as the couples kissed, making their vows official. They walked out and noticed all the familiar faces they'd come to know since they'd been on their journey—Melissa, Judith, James, and Vincent. Judith and James had come as each other's plus ones.

Jason and Amanda were behind bars for years for stalking, rape, kidnapping, and intimidation. Ray and Stella were finally at ease.

They all agreed that their first dance should be to "Here and Now" by Luther Vandross. They were introduced at the reception, and Stella came out in a more comfortable fitted dress with custom-made white Jordans with diamonds. She wanted to dance all night. Kayla wore the same dress but with real shoes. The song started playing, and both couples looked into each other's eyes.

Ray held Stella tight. She leaned back and mouthed the words to the song. Everybody was singing along. They decided to get the babies involved. Ray grabbed Ruben, and Seb grabbed Corina, and they all danced and sang together.

It was a beautiful picture. Corina was all smiles like her mommy and daddy. Ruben was still too small to understand what was going on. Stella grabbed her phone to get their picture. One picture of both of them holding Ruben and smiling and one of them holding him and kissing his cheeks.

Ray reached over and gave Seb a fist bump. Kayla and Stella hugged. They were exactly where they needed and wanted to be, with the people they wanted to be with. They couldn't have written it any better themselves.

A Week Later

The six of them sat on the beach in San Juan. When they had decided on the date for the wedding, they had also decided they wanted to go somewhere warm for their honeymoon. What better place than the homeland? Even though Kay was Costa Rican, she had grown up with Puerto Ricans, and hanging with Stella had Kay threatening Seb with her *chancla* whenever they argued.

The ocean was beautiful here. The water was blue, and you could see the bottom. Not like Coney Island, they thought.

Kay and Seb looked at each other and smiled. Little Corina had her little bathing suit on and looked so cute.

Ray and Stella had baby Ruben in between them on his back. Thankfully, he was a good baby and didn't cry much. Ray and Seb got up and went to the bartender. The babies were not on breast milk so Stella and Kay were enjoying the hell out of this trip. As they were walking away, Kay and Stella admired their men. Good Lord, they were fine. They came back with four tequila shots. They held the shots up. Ray looked around and smiled. "To the future," he said. They repeated after him.

"To the future!"

About the Author

K. Cruz was born in Brooklyn, New York, to Puerto Rican parents, Raul and Maria. She currently resides in New Jersey with her husband, Luis and three fur babies, Gizmo, Penny, and Raven. Her hobbies include collecting Funko Pops, watching *The Golden Girls*, reading, watching fantasy shows / movies, and listening to music. *Stella & Ray: A Nuyorican Love Story* is her first novel.